To the Murphy Family —

Great neighbors

& a fabulous dog!
(Saw this book and knew it was Brian!)

See you in the

Spring!

Robert + Barbara

BALL

Word and pictures by Mary Sullivan

Houghton Mifflin Harcourt Books for Children

HOUGHTON MIFFLIN HARCOURT

Boston New York

For Scout . . . the best dog ever in the whole wide world.
I miss you.

Houghton Mifflin Books for Children is an imprint of
Houghton Mifflin Harcourt Publishing Company.

www.hmhbooks.com

The text of this book is set in Myriad Tilt.
The illustrations are pencil on Strathmore drawing paper, scanned and digitally colored.

ISBN 978-0-547-75936-4

Manufactured in China
SCP 10 9 8 7 6 5 4 3 2
4500413955

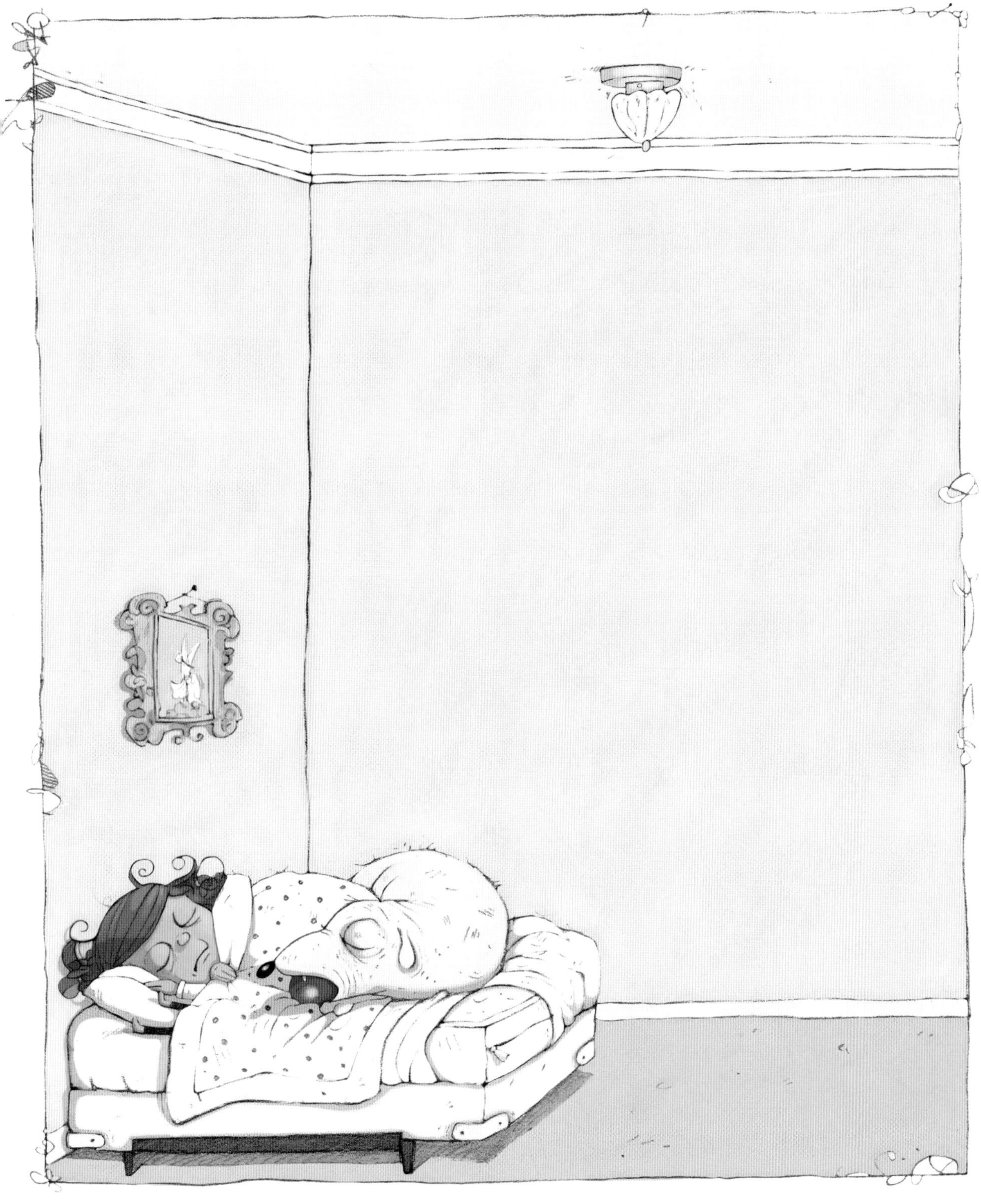

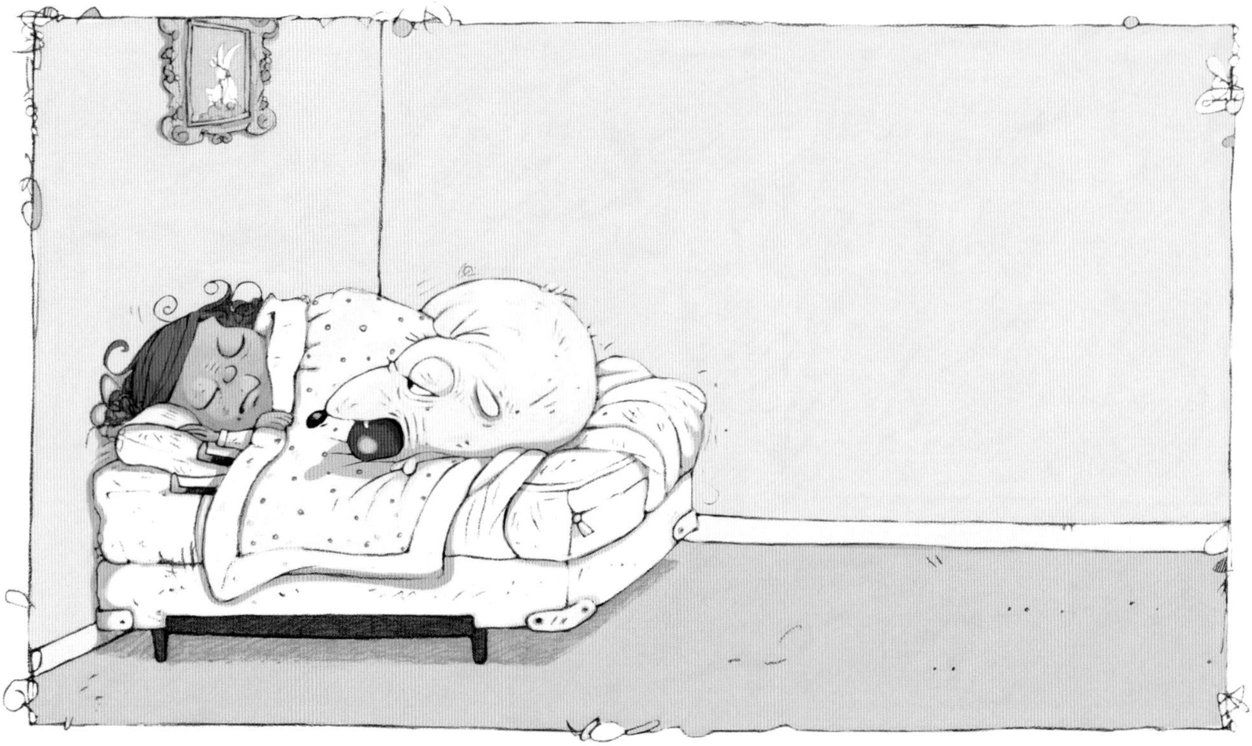

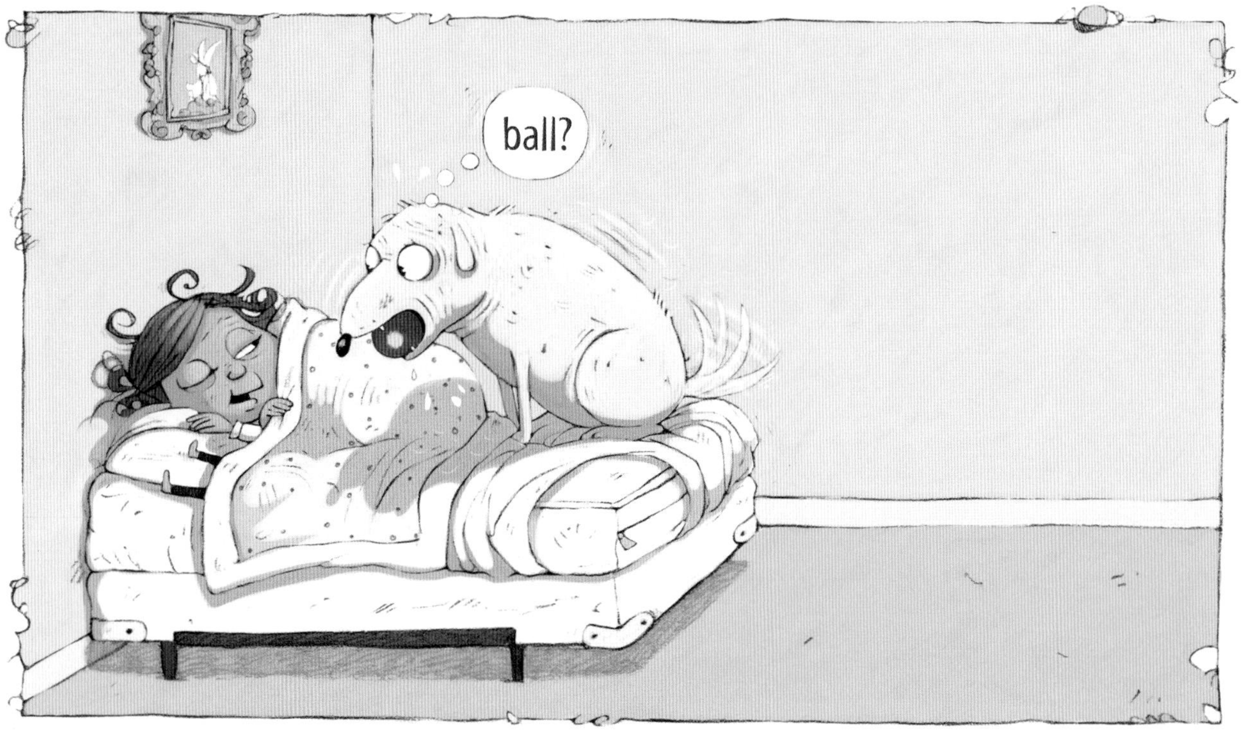
ball?

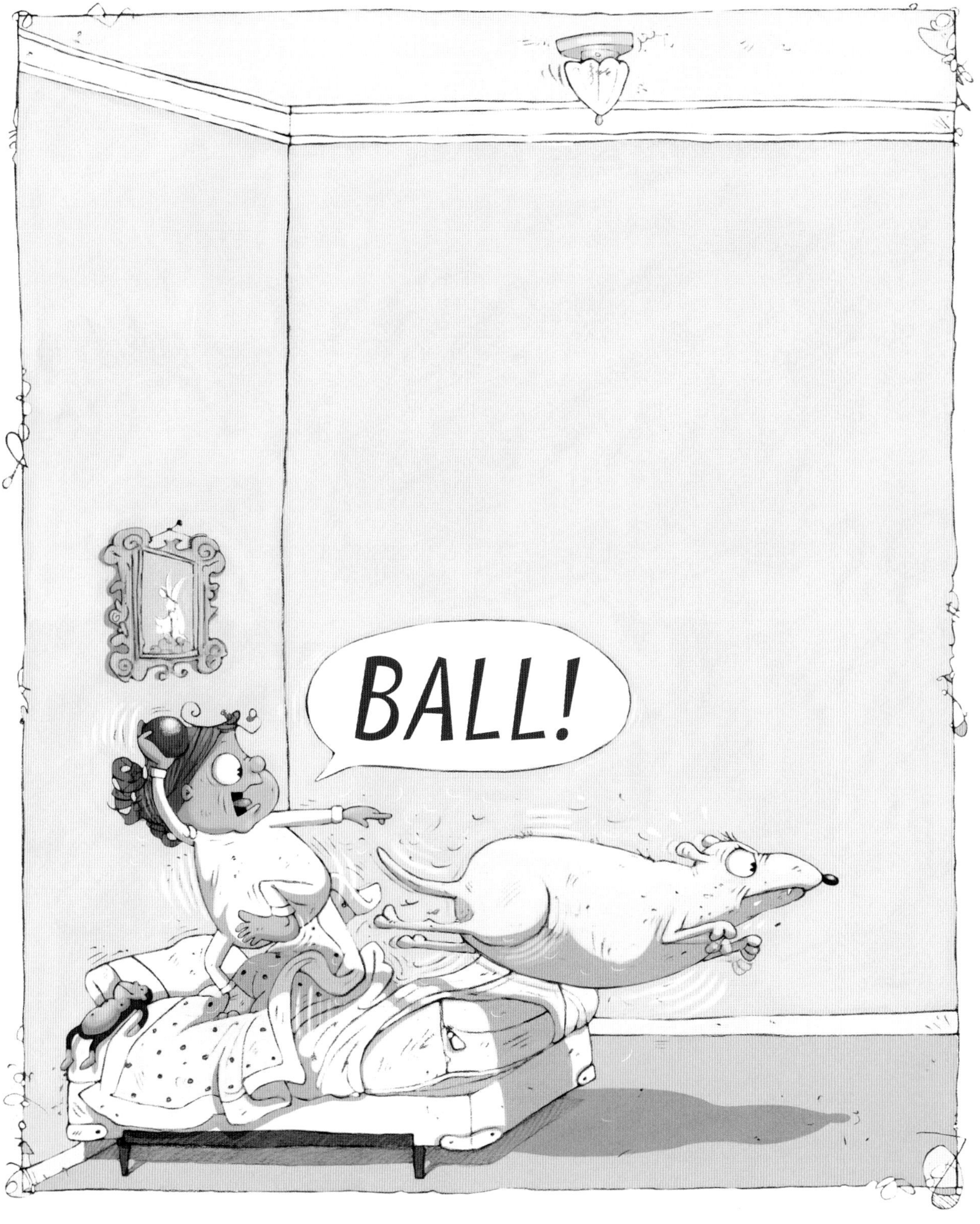
BALL!

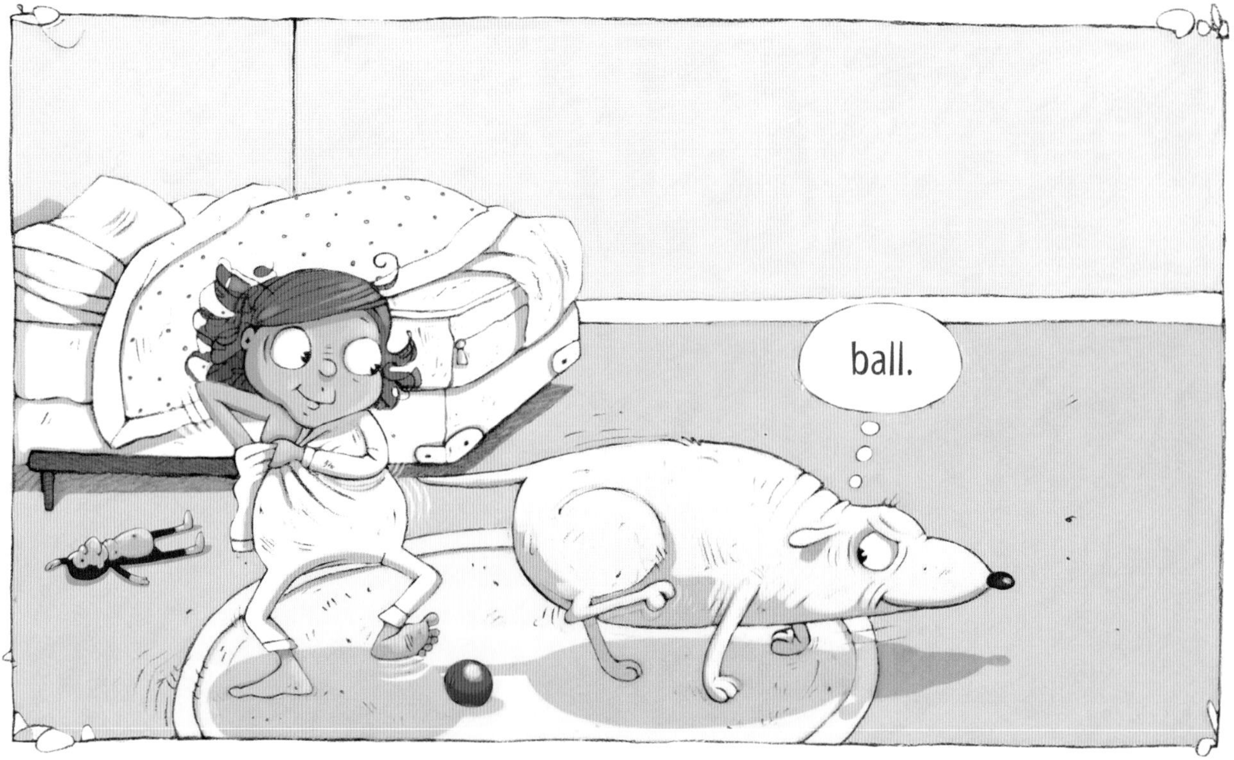
ball.

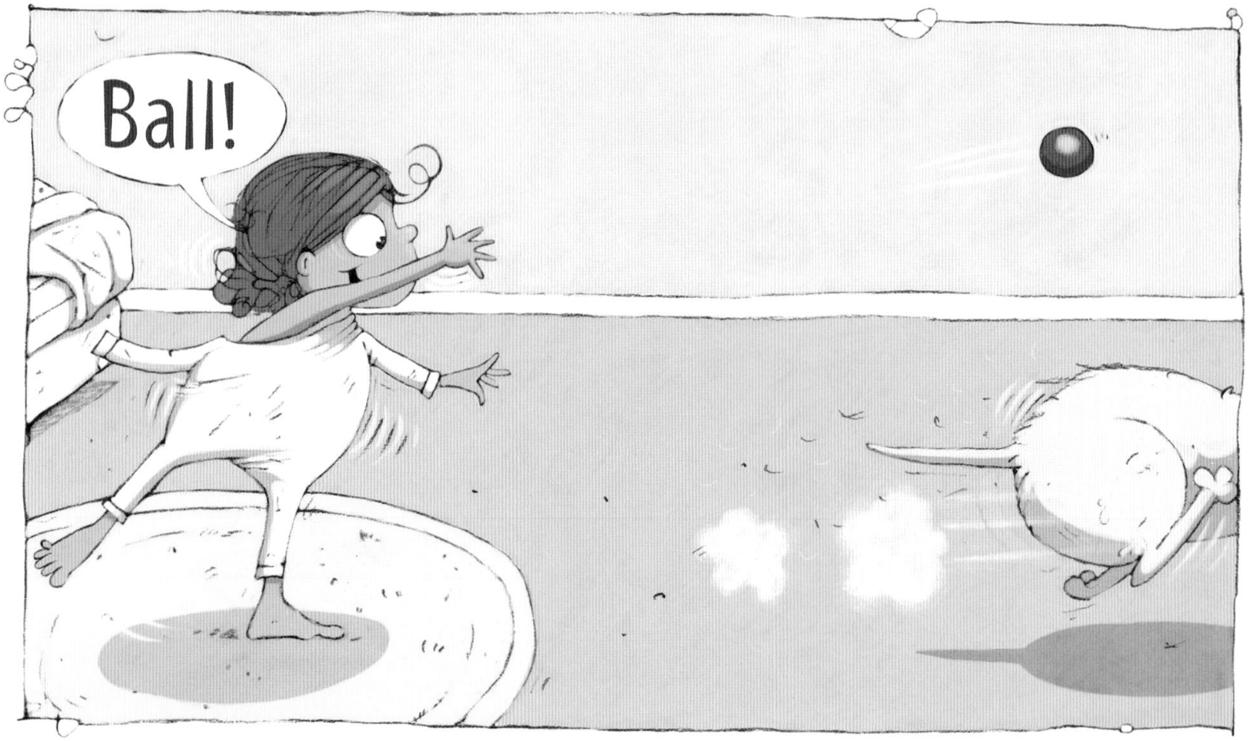
Ball!

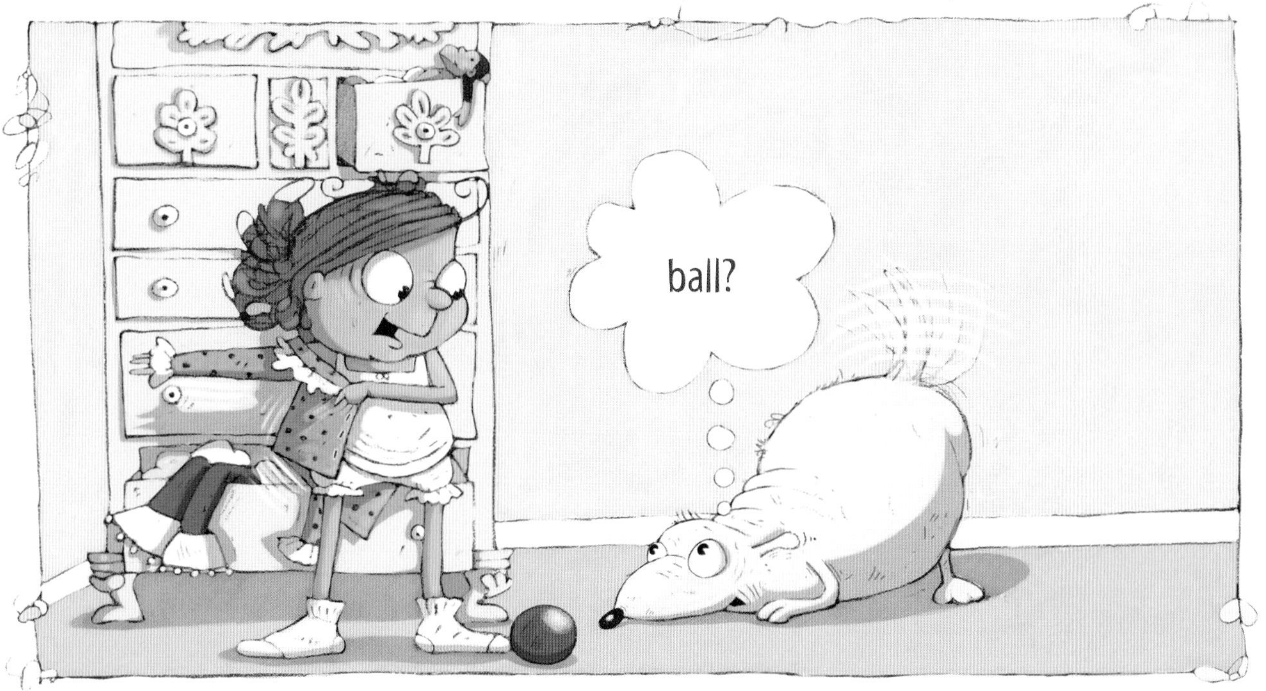
ball?

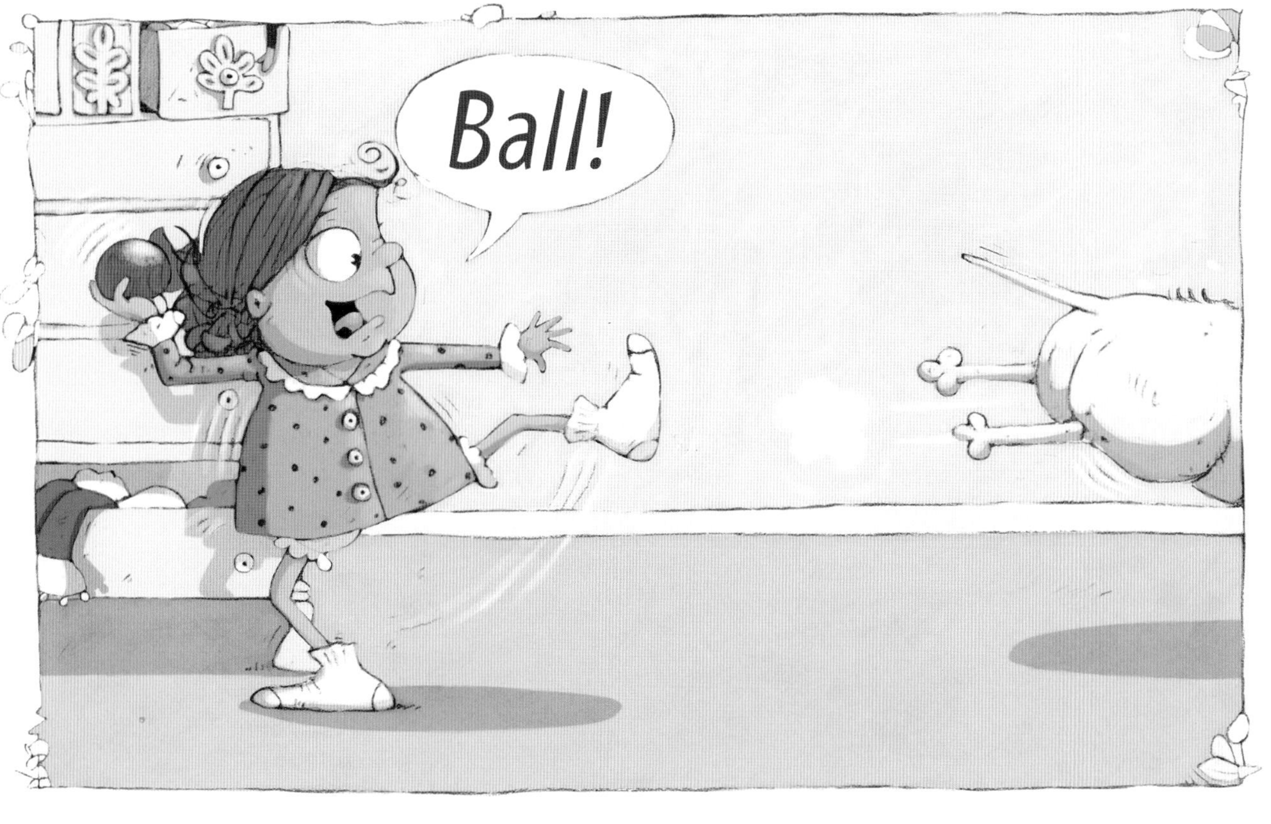
Ball!

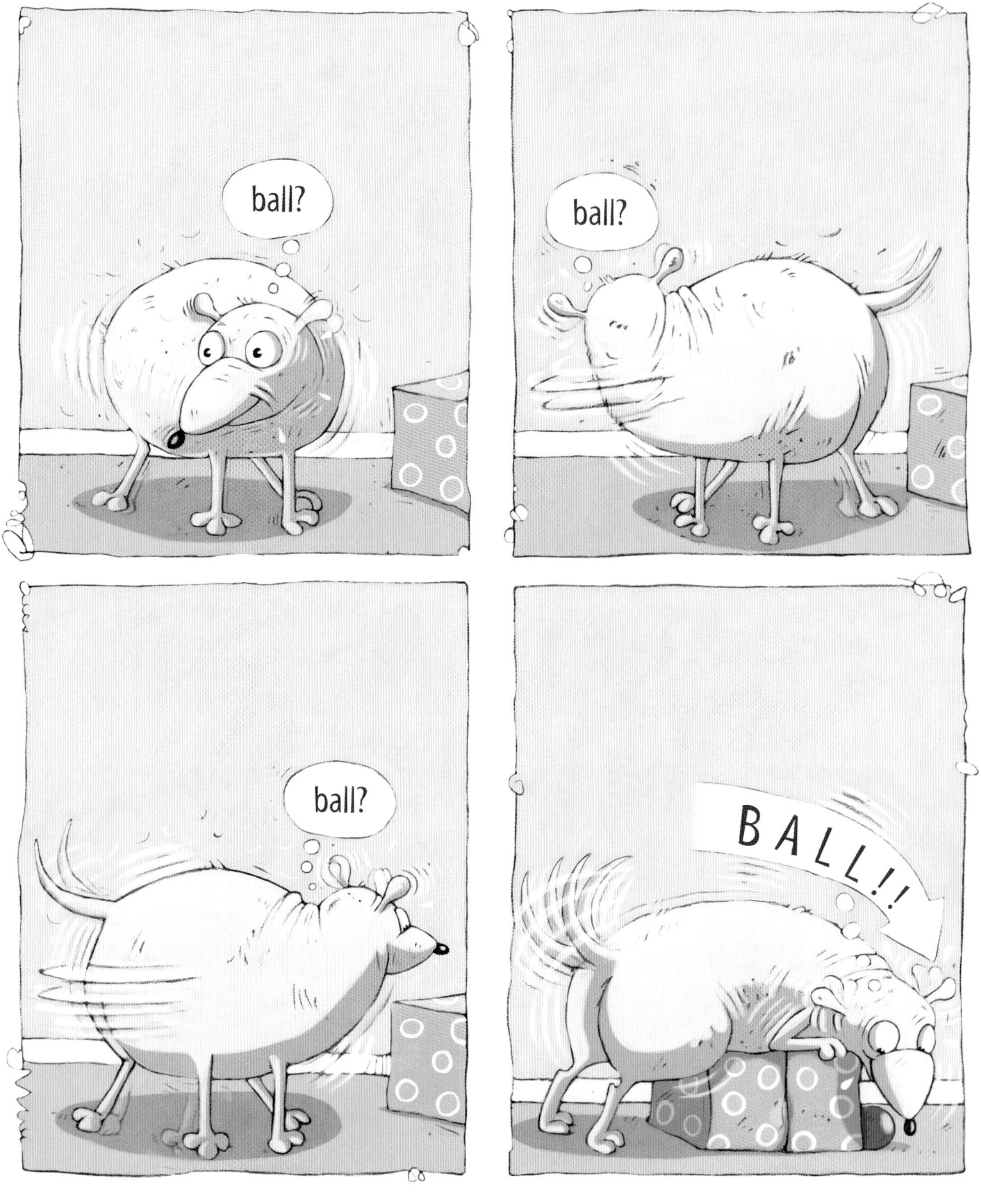
ball?
ball?
ball?
BALL!!

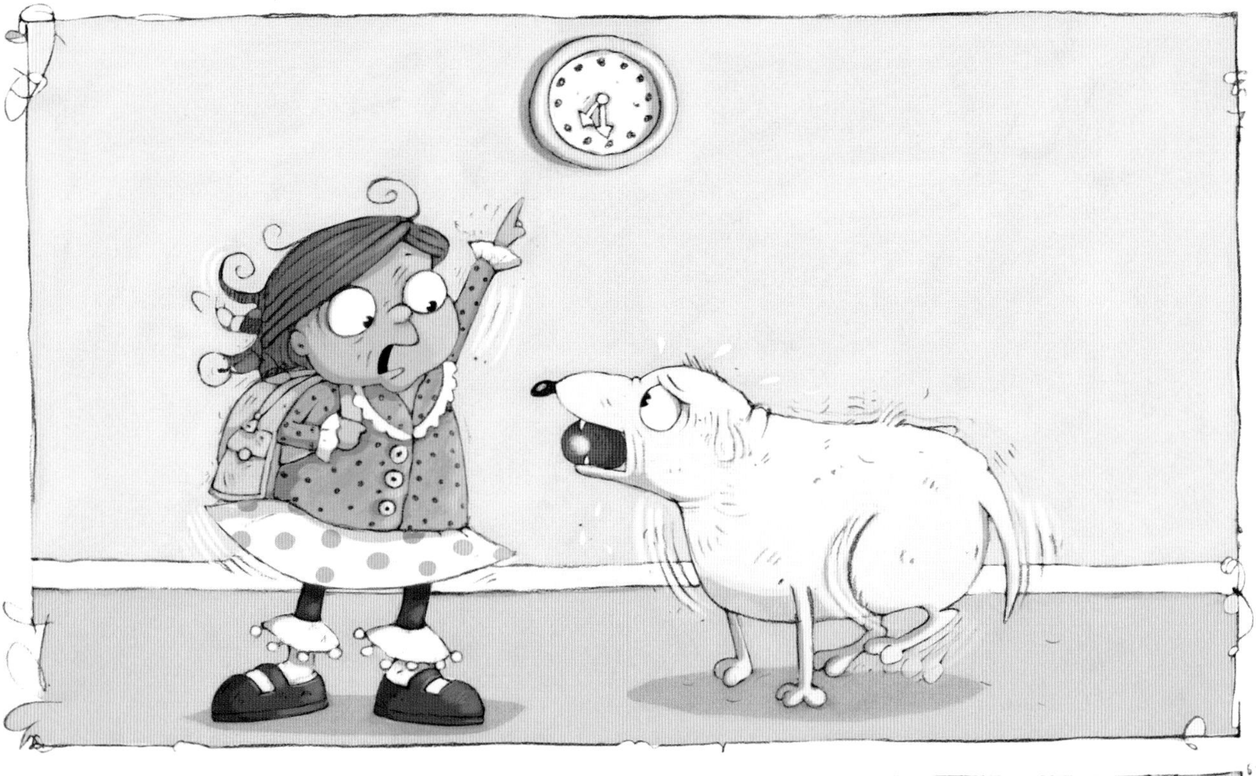

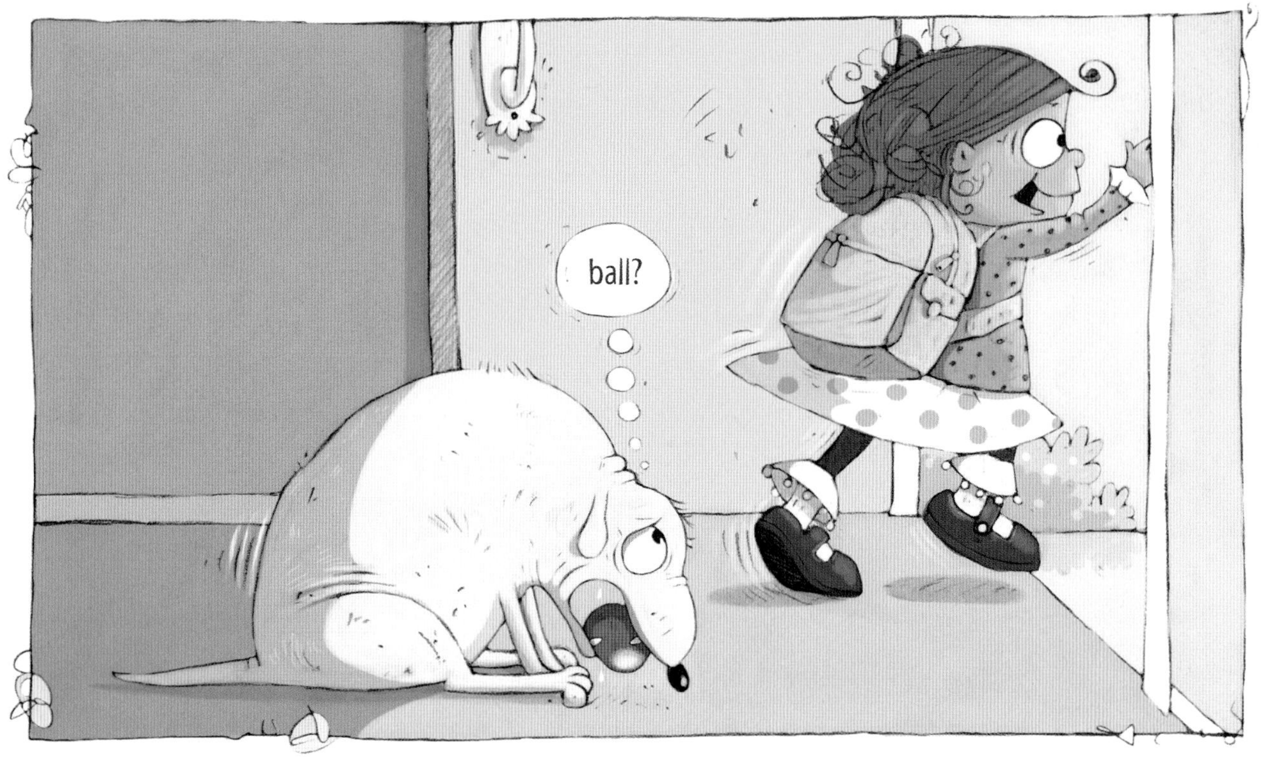
ball?

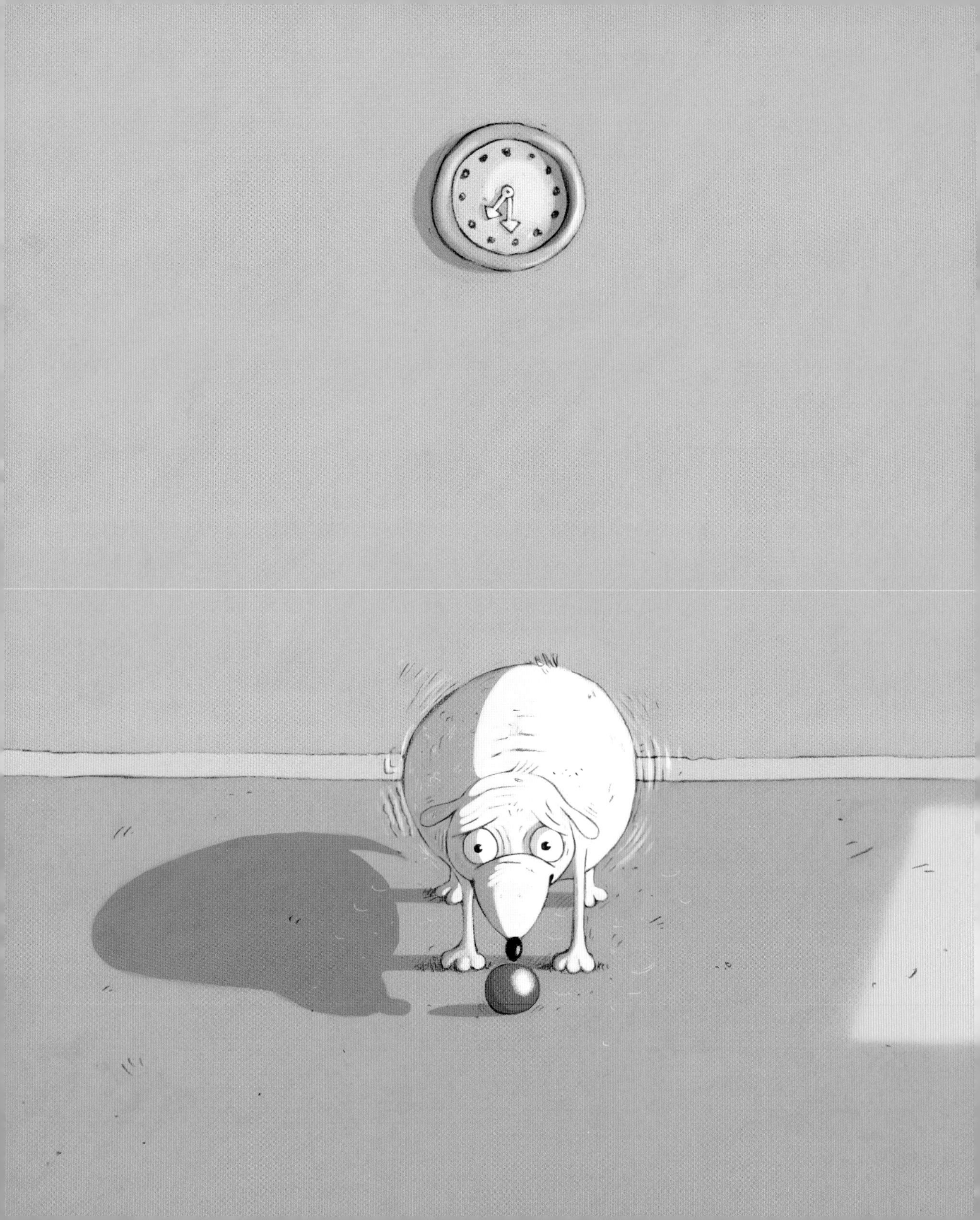

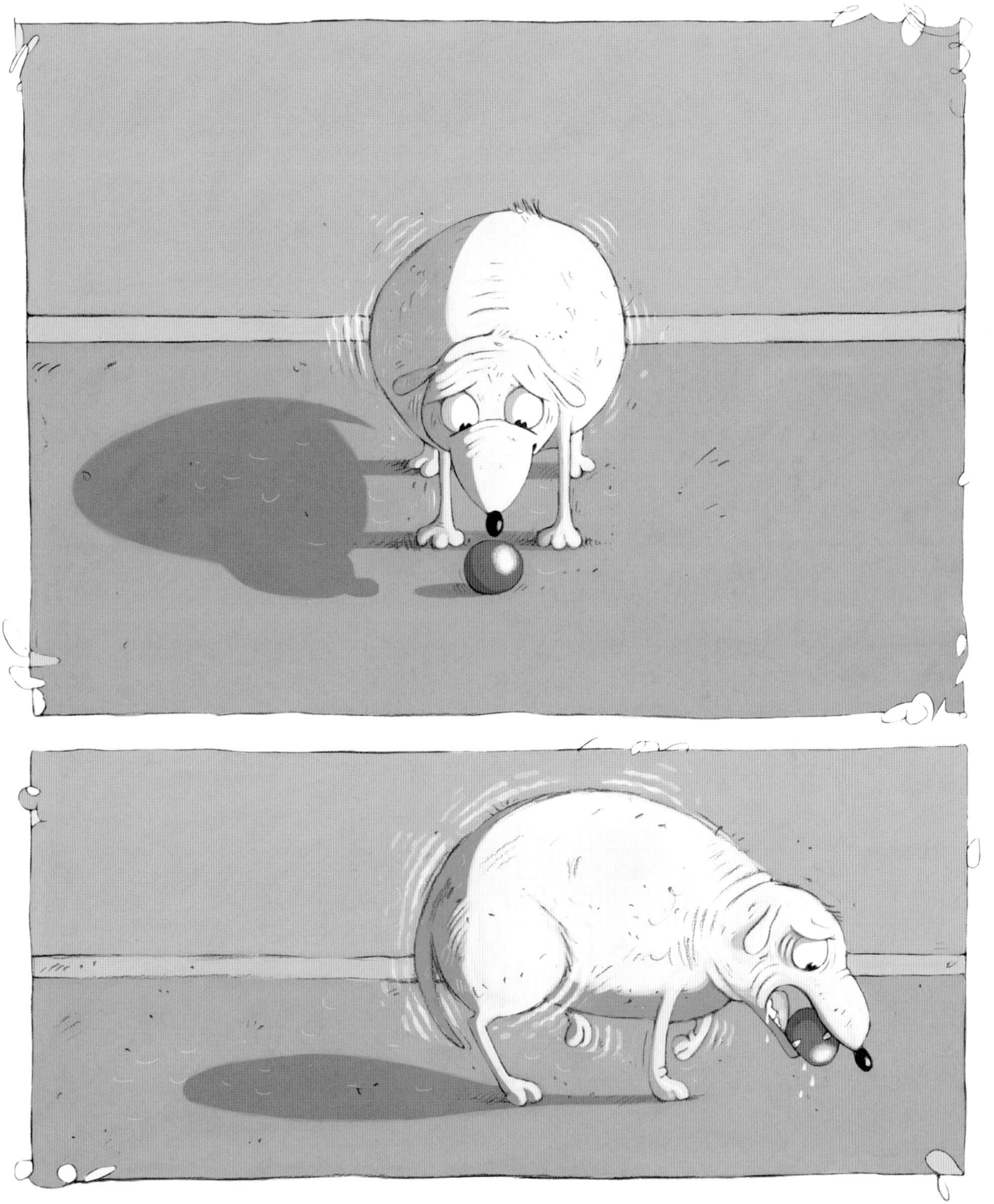

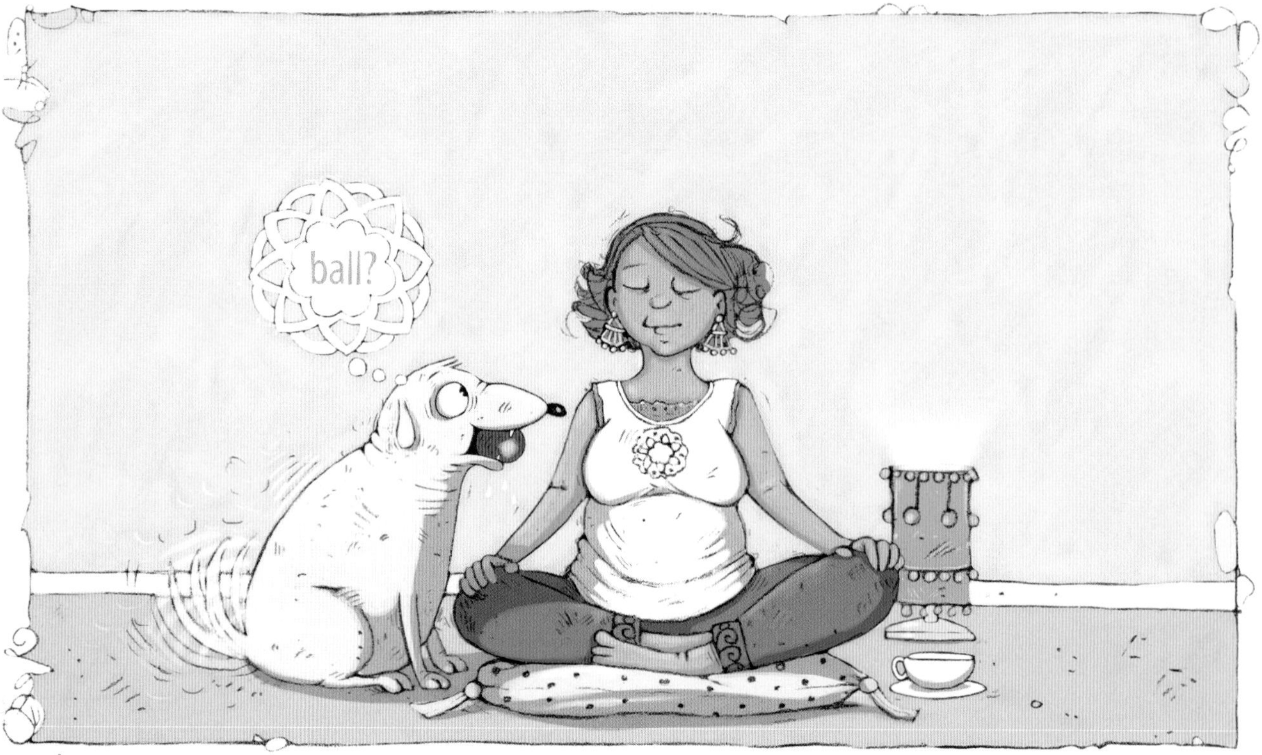
ball?

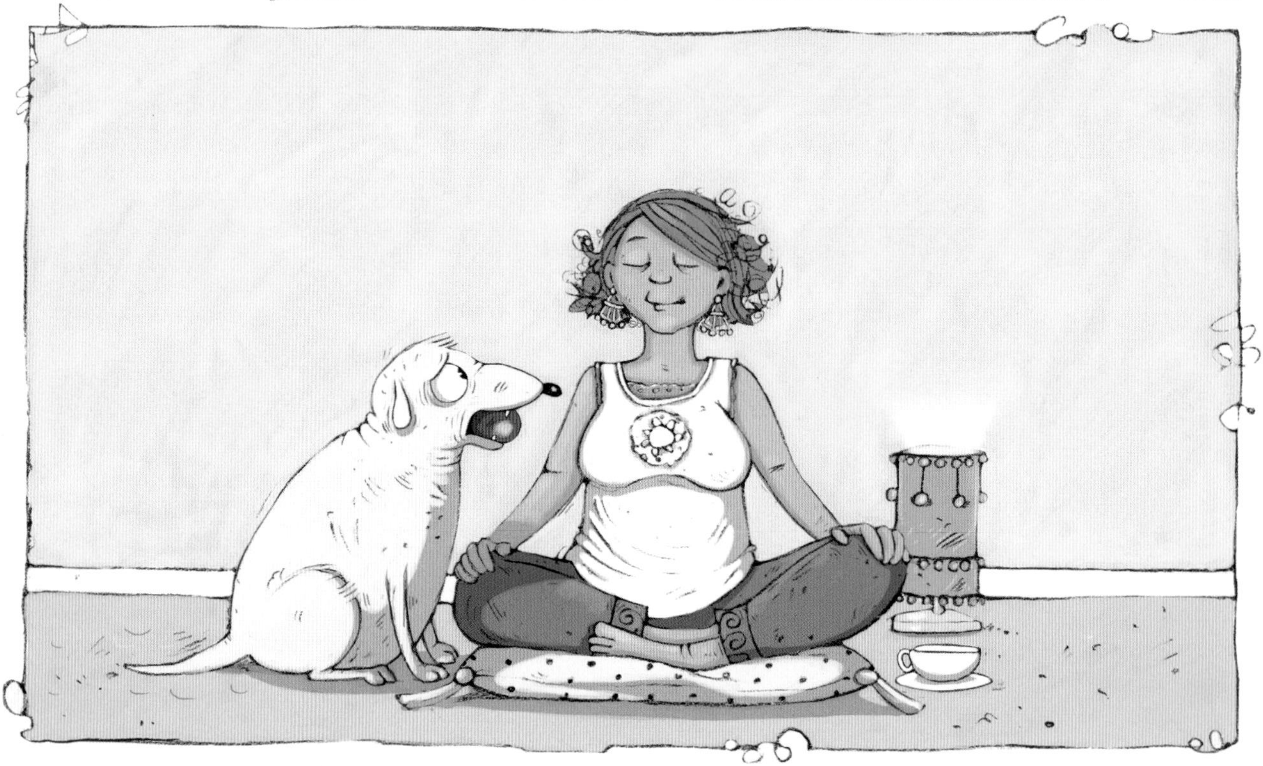

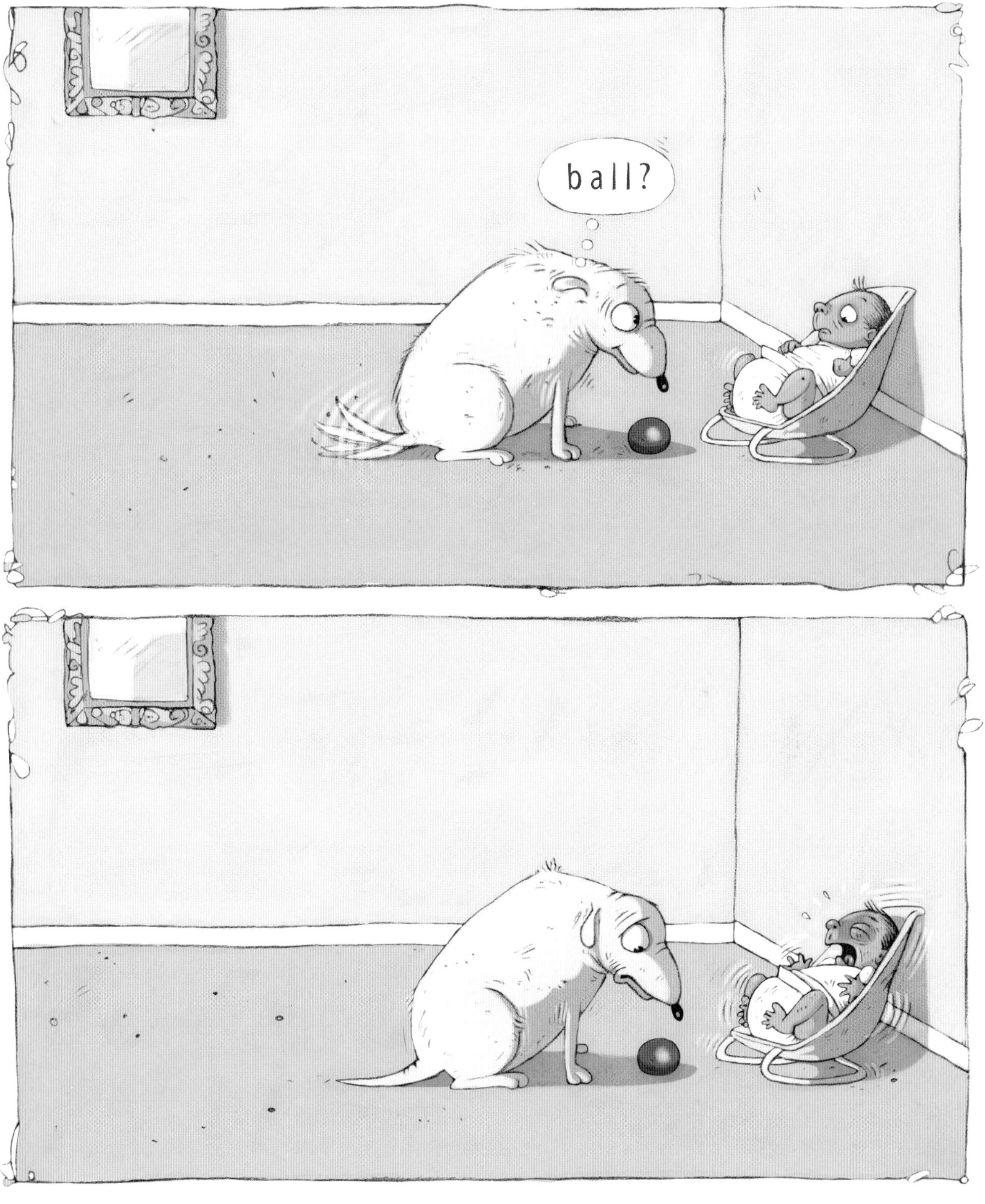
ball?

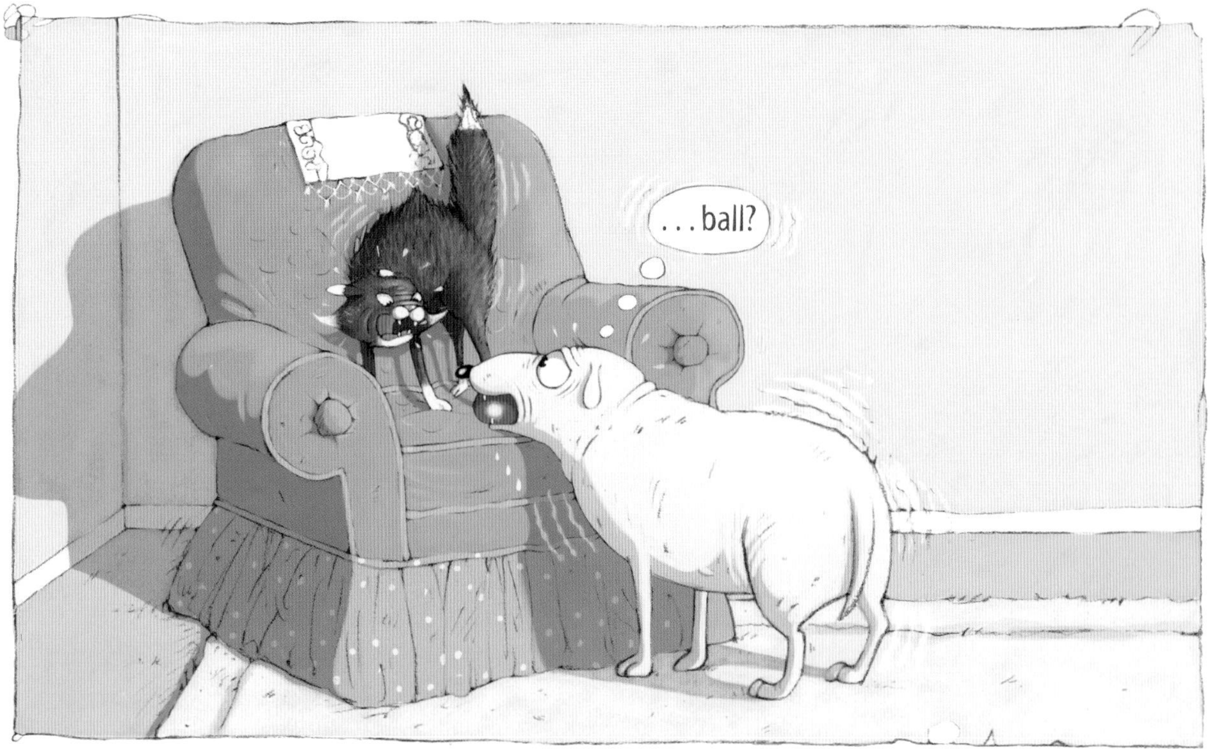
. . . ball?

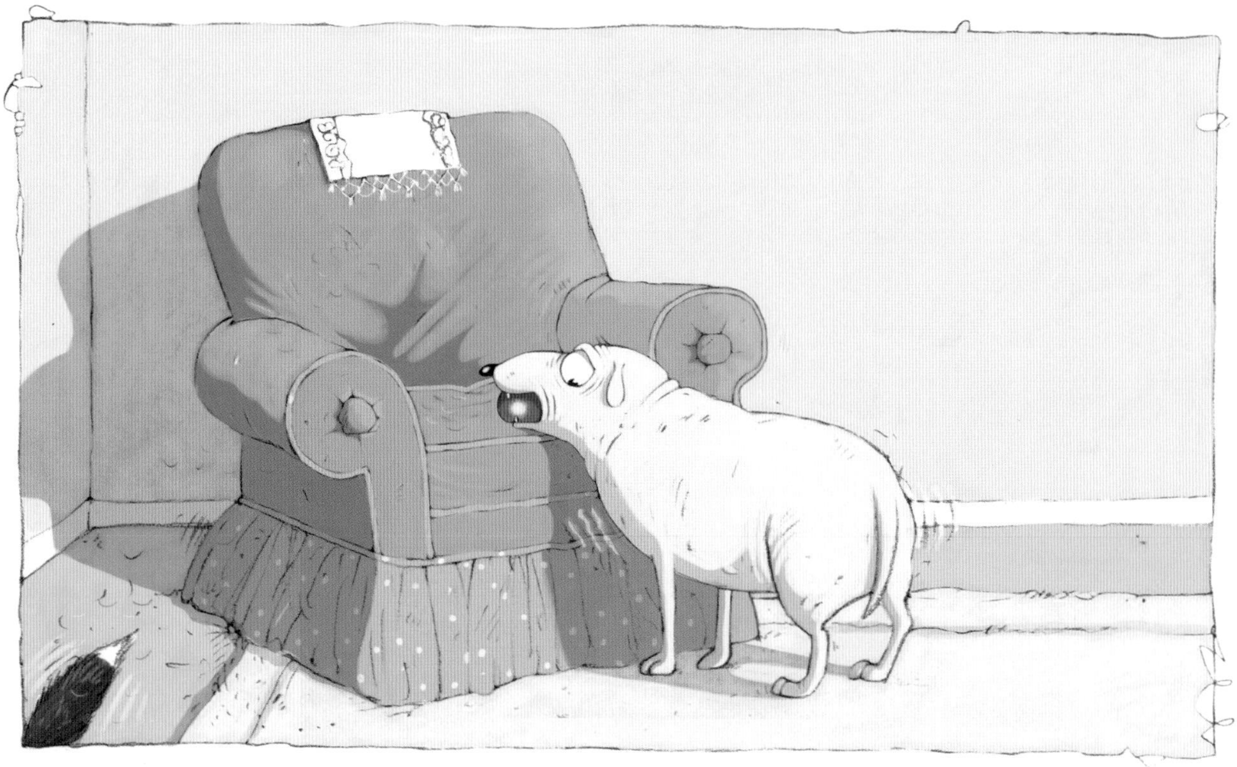

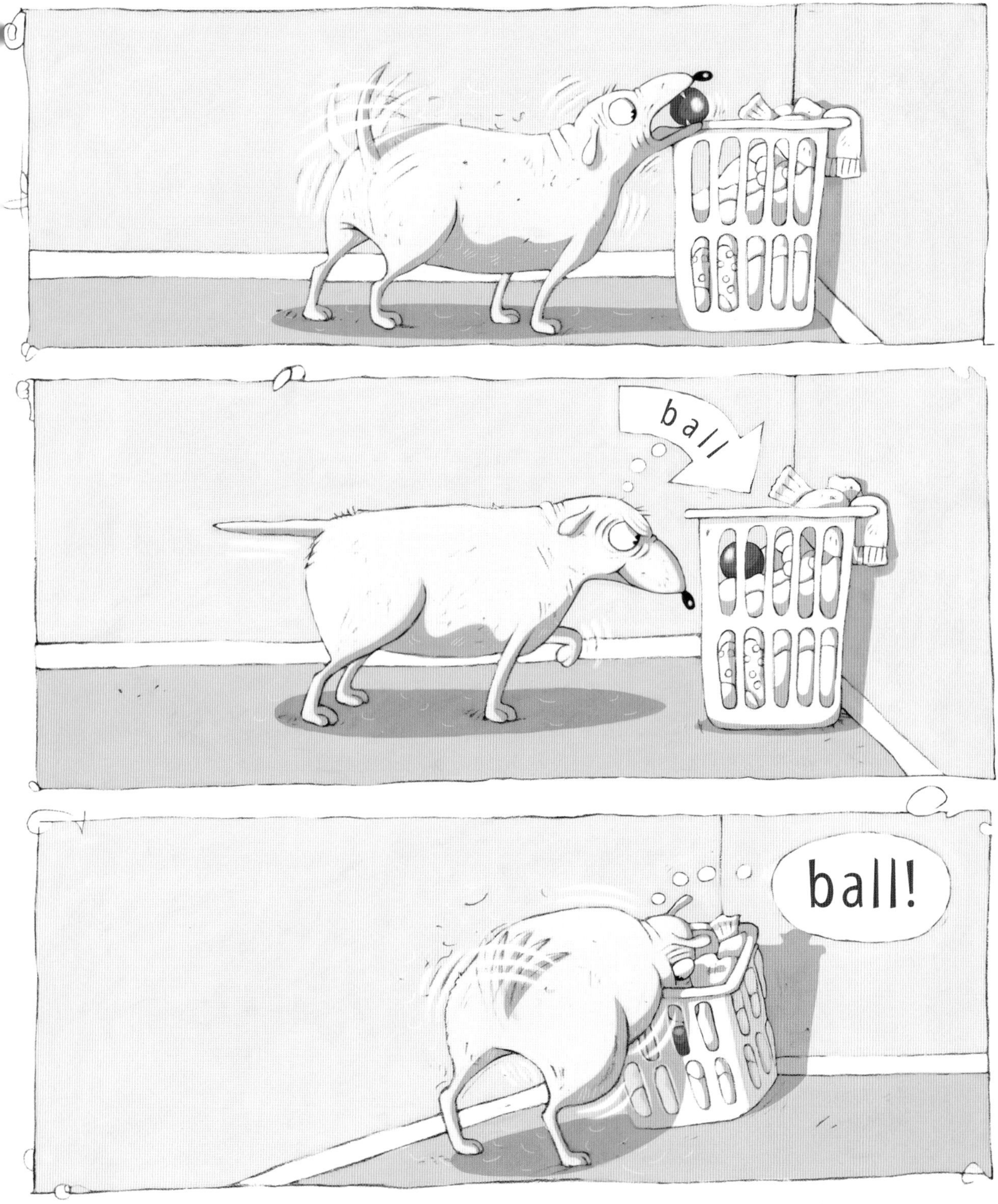
ball
ball!

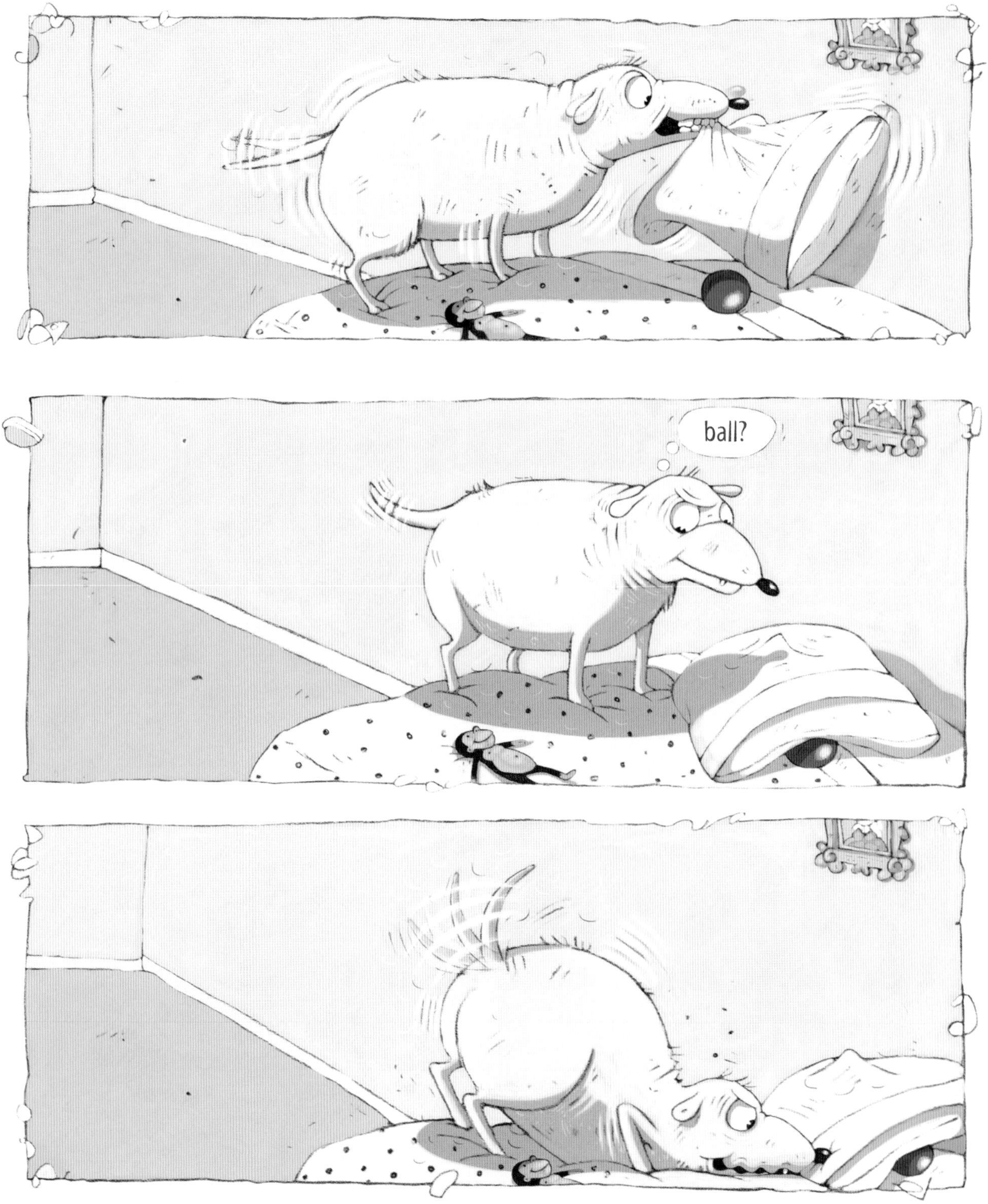
ball?

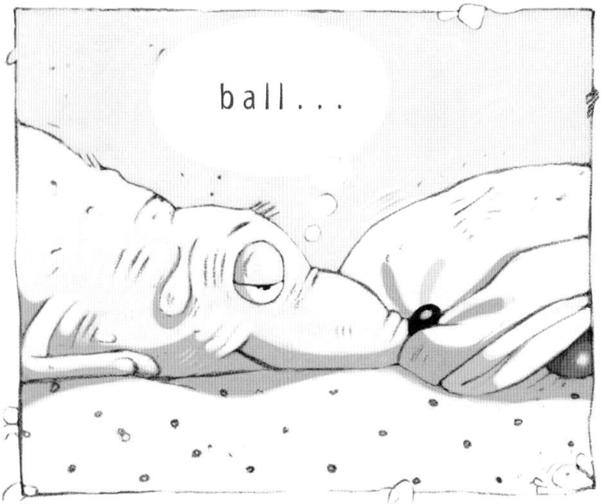
ball...

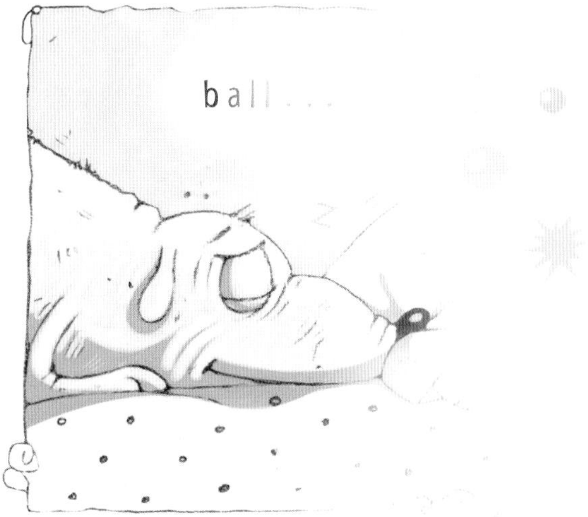
ball...

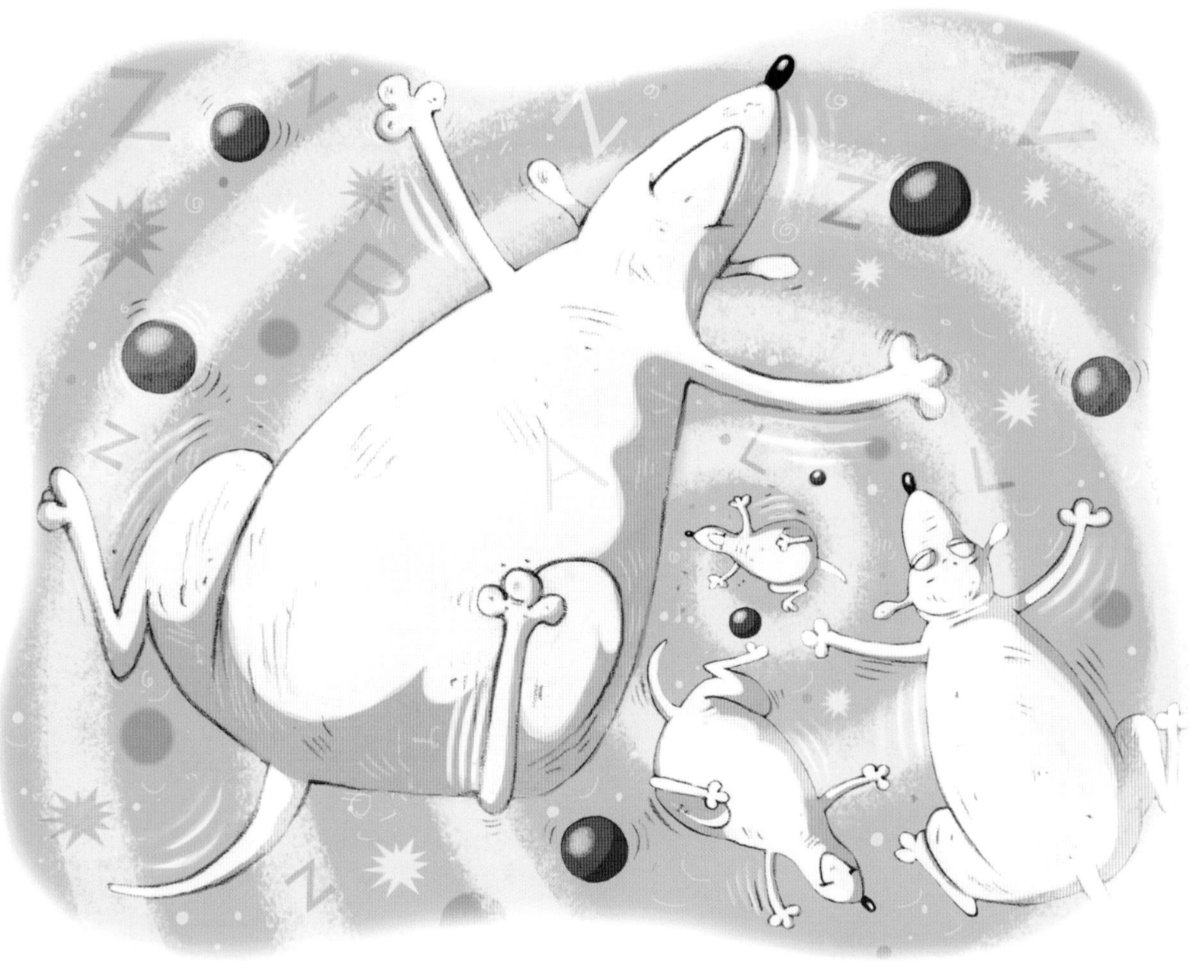

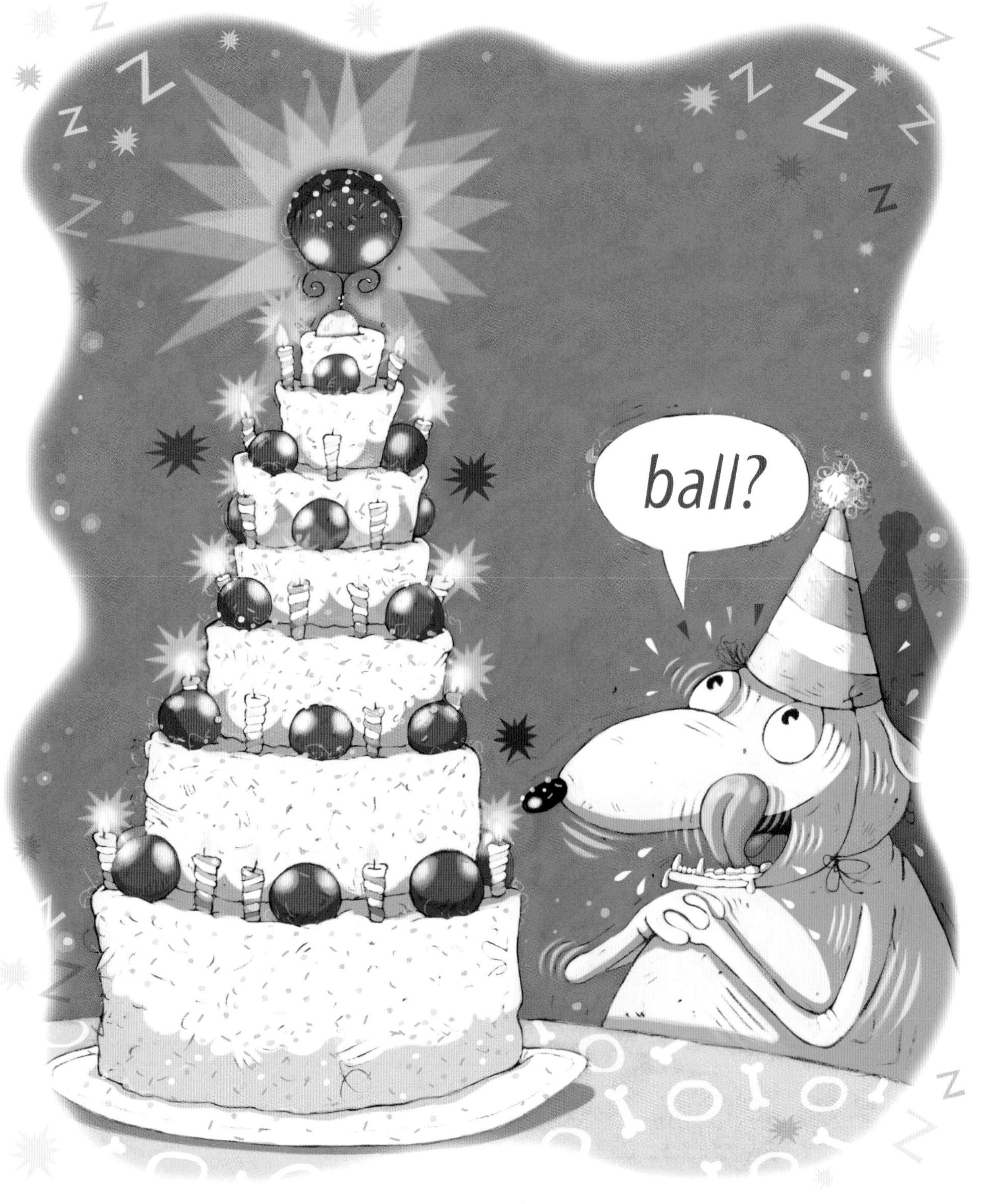
ball?
Z Z Z

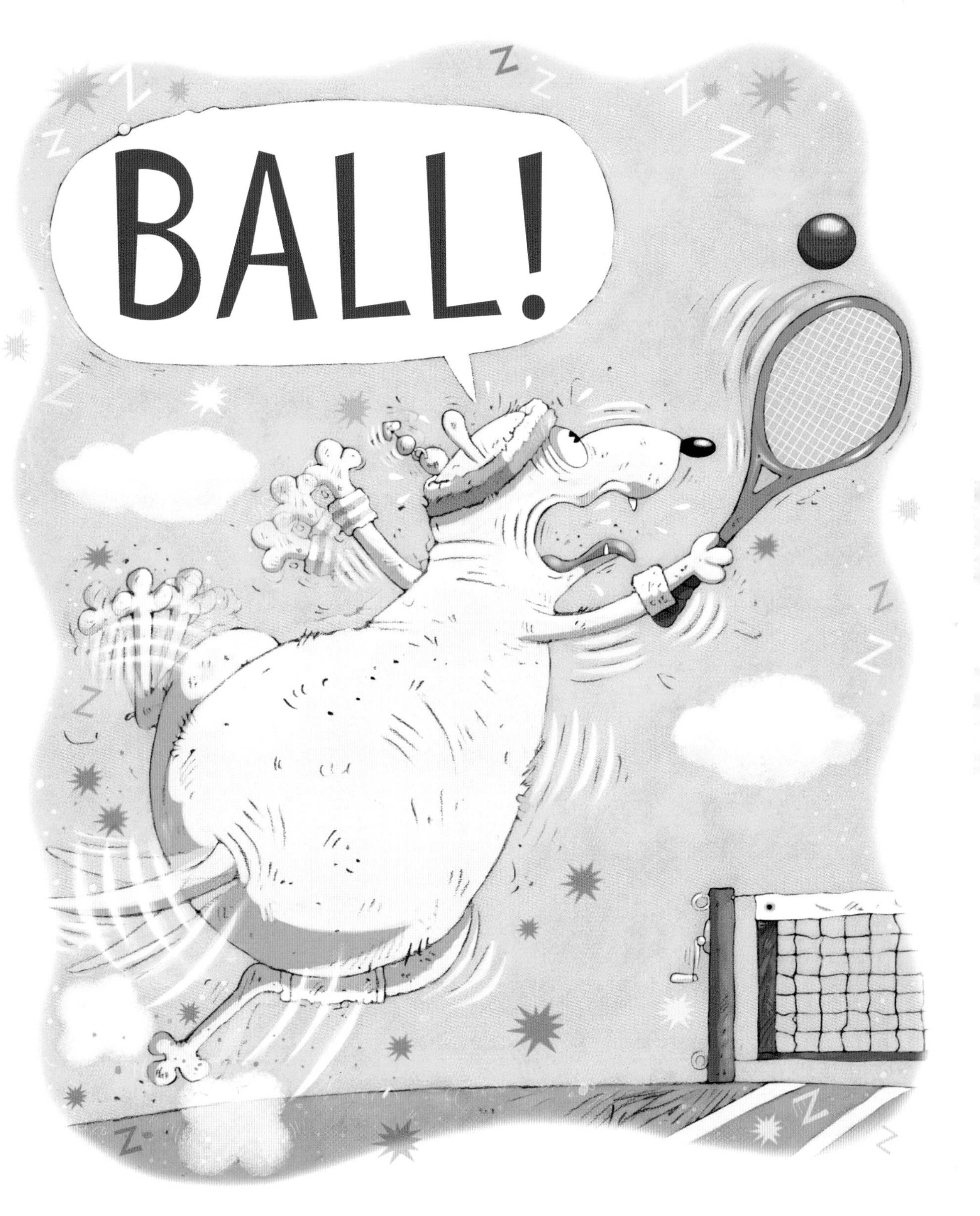
BALL!

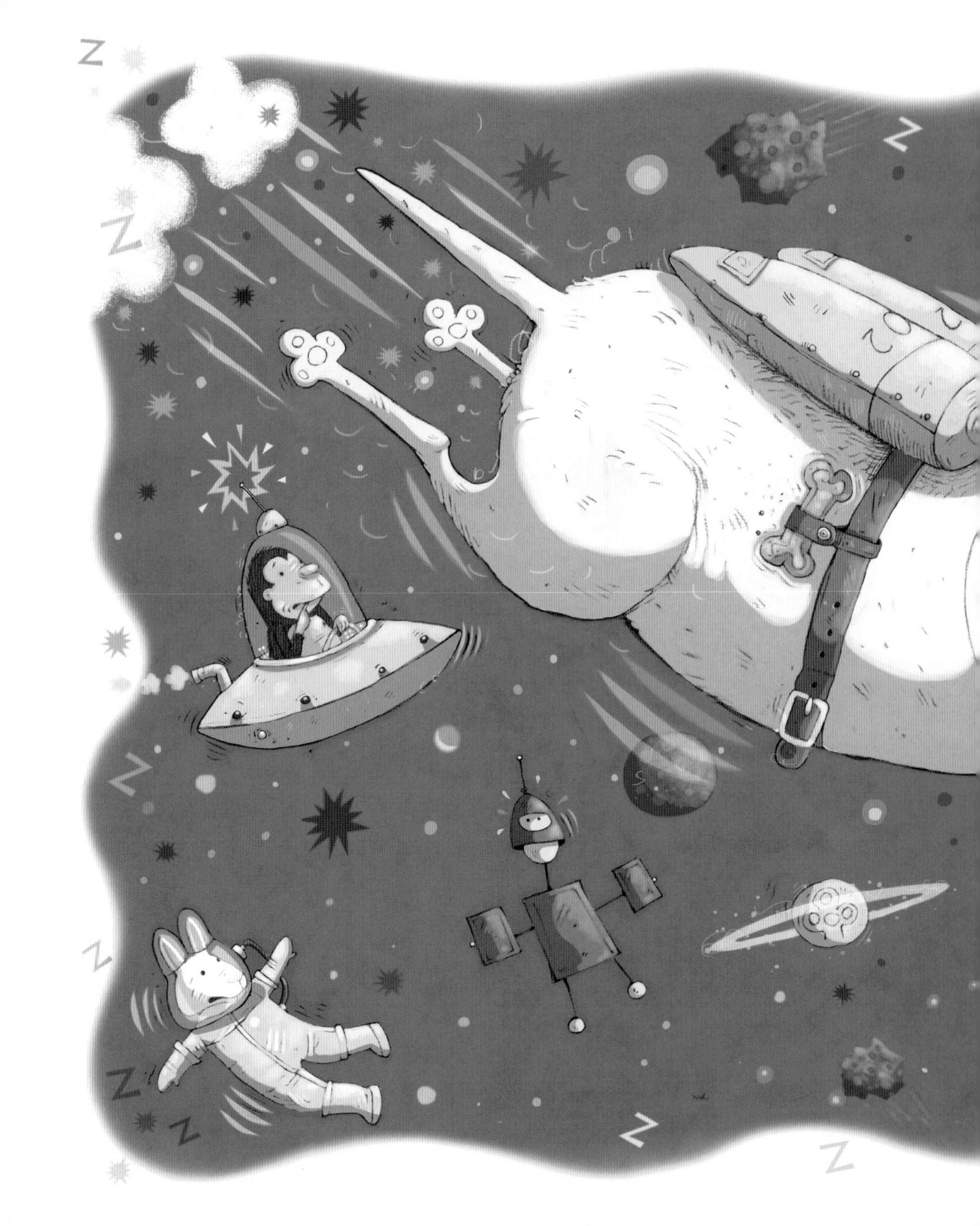

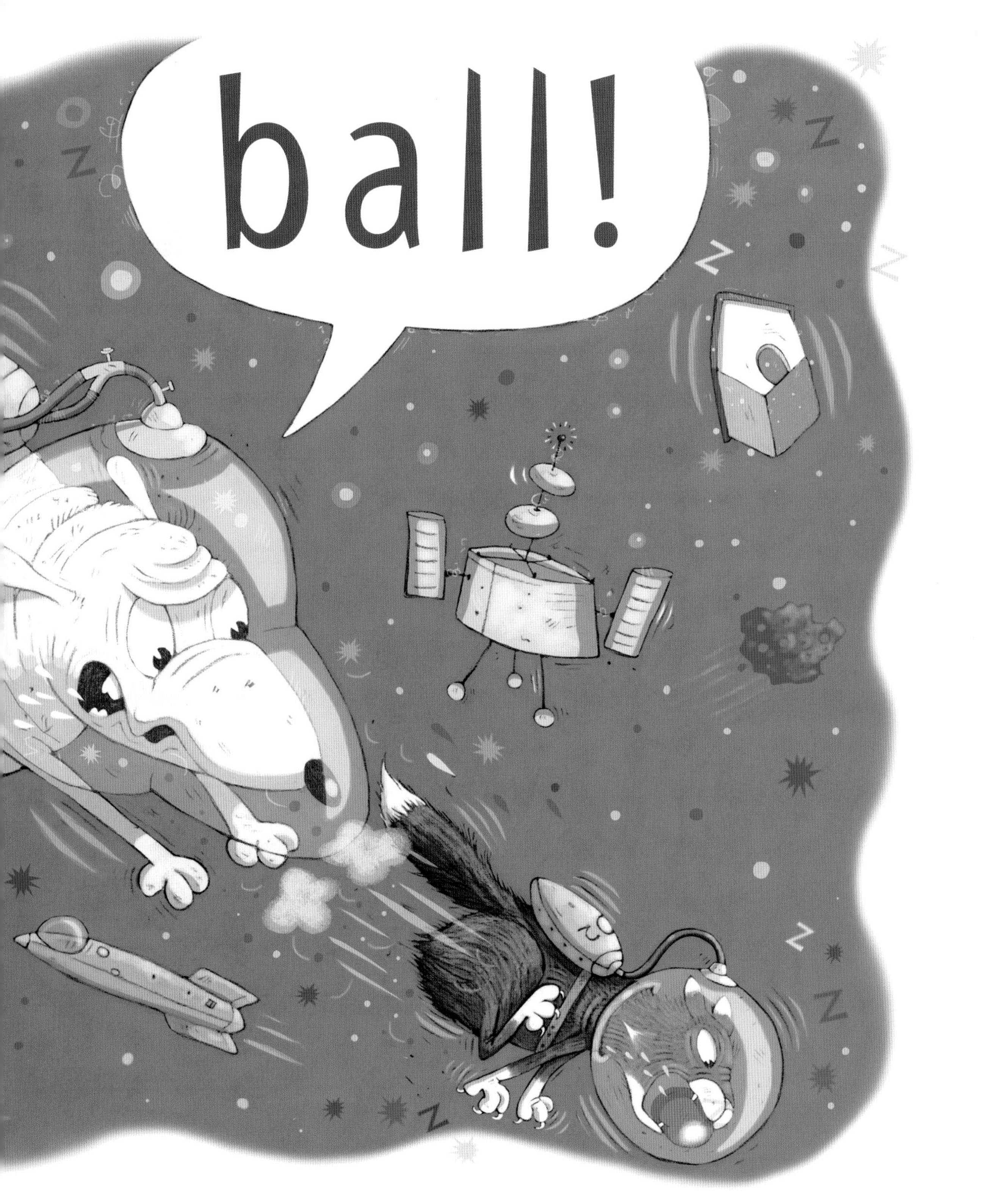
ball!

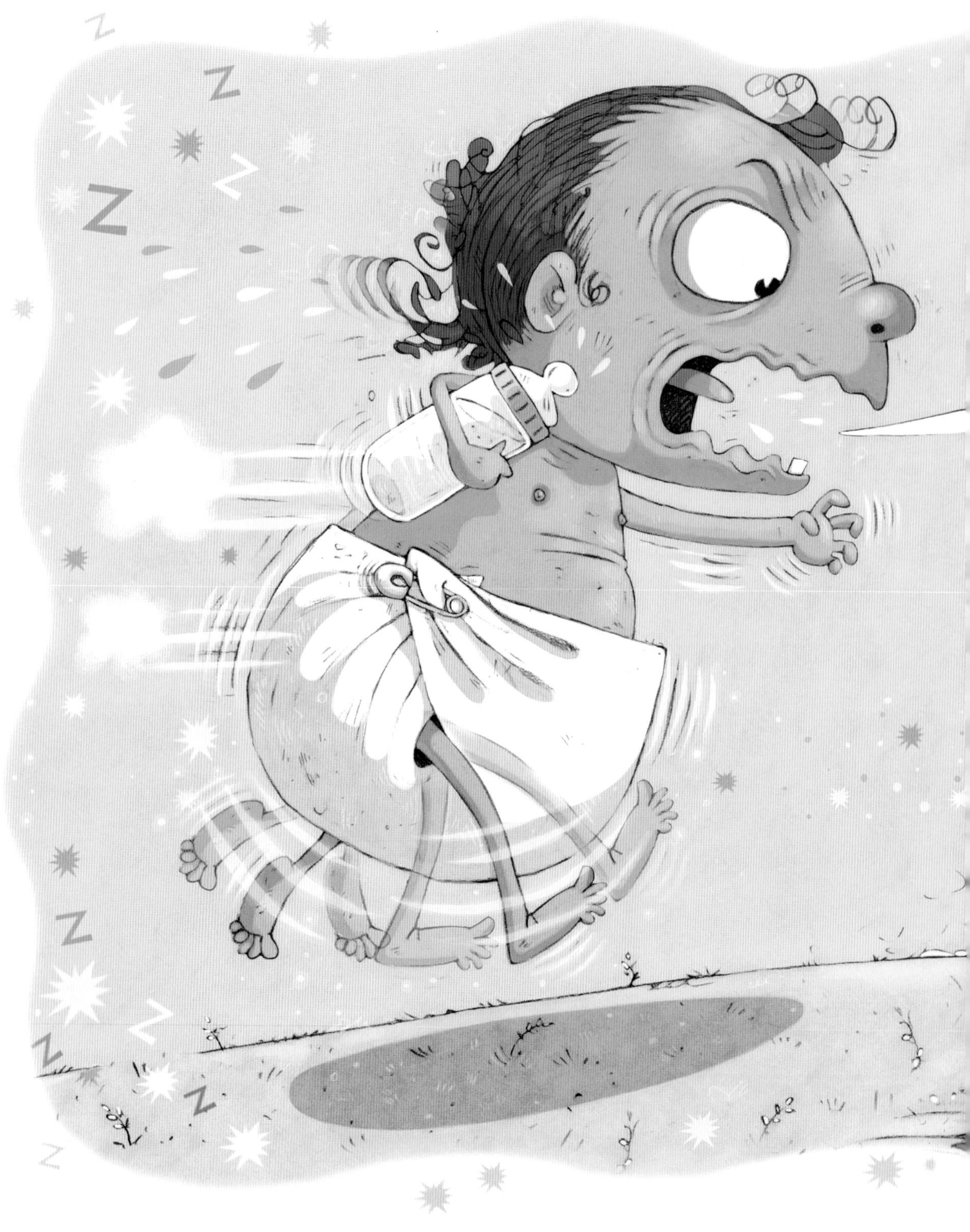

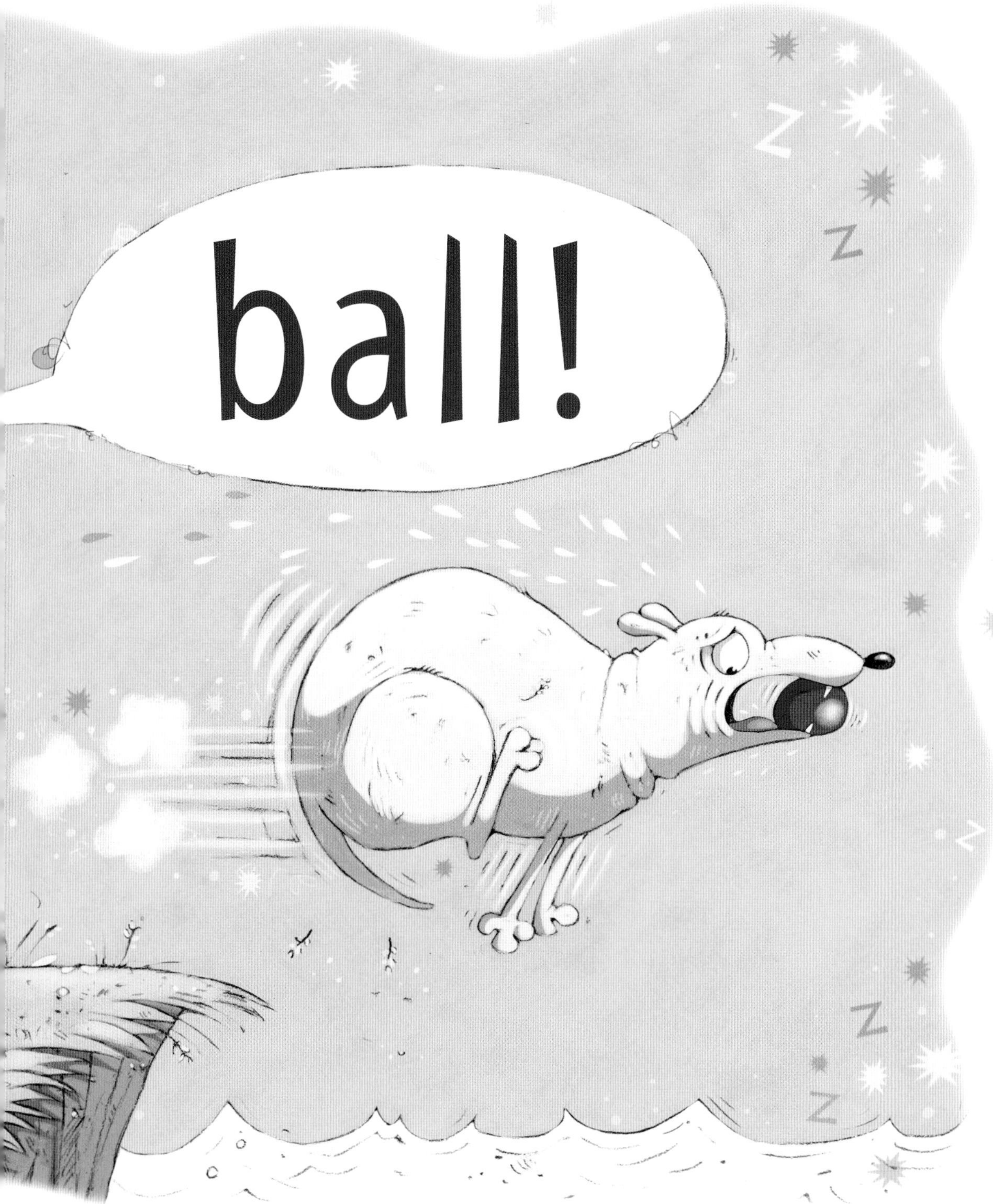
ball!

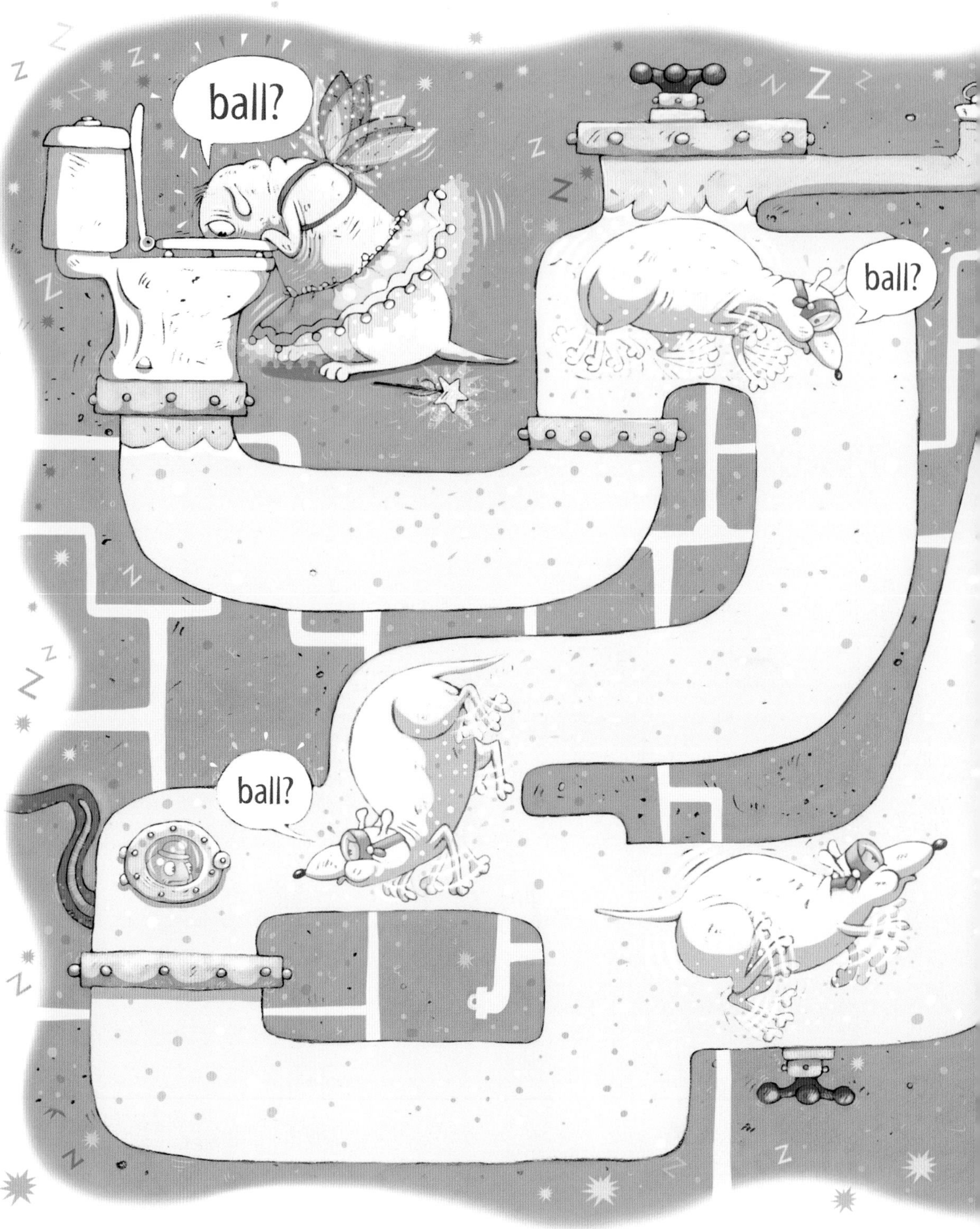
ball?
ball?
ball?

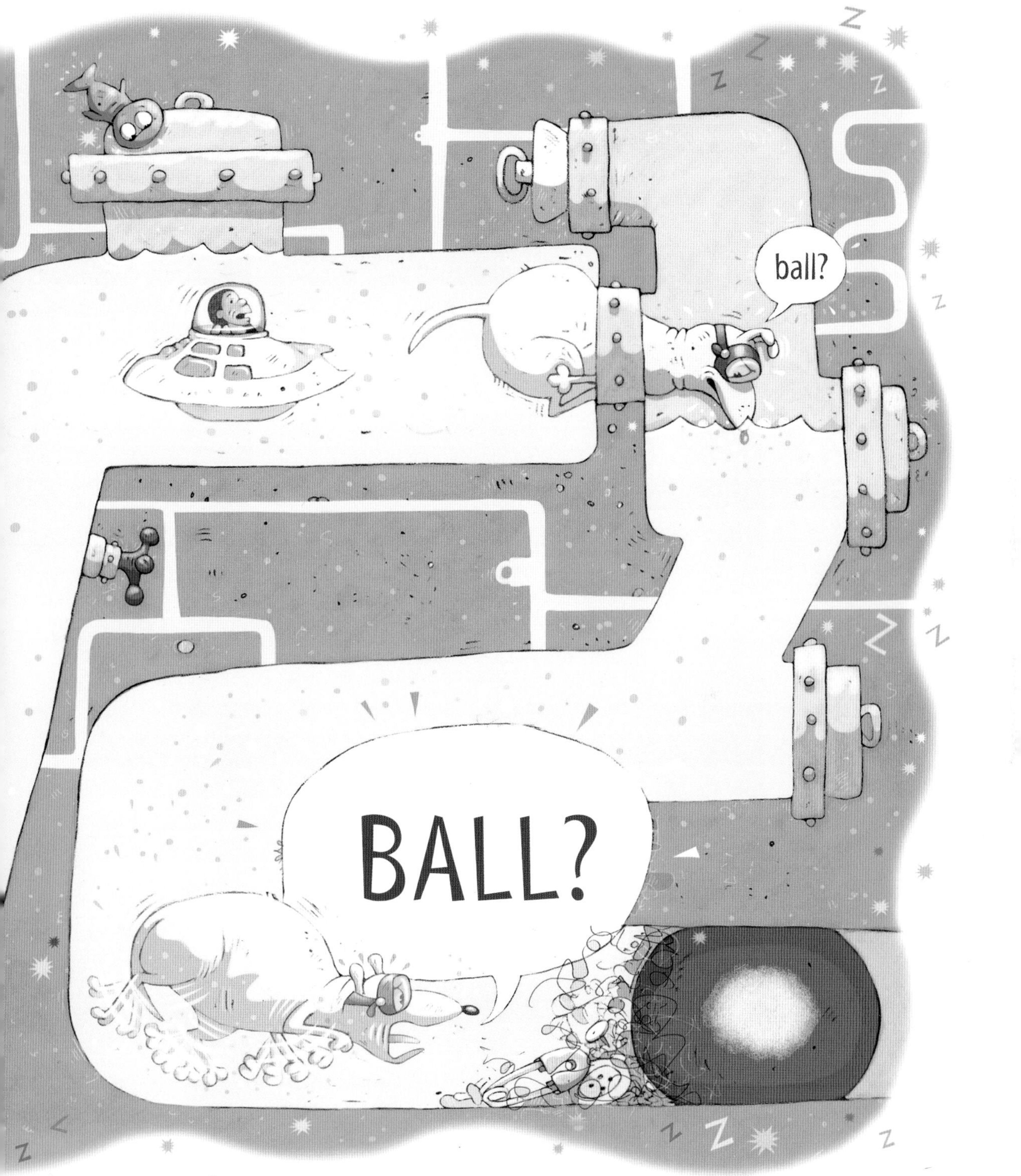
ball?
BALL?

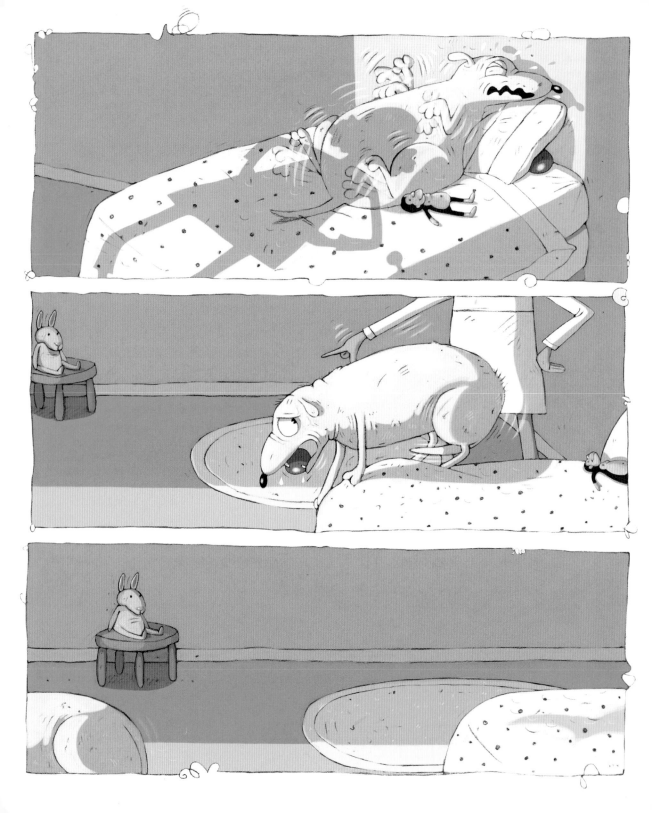

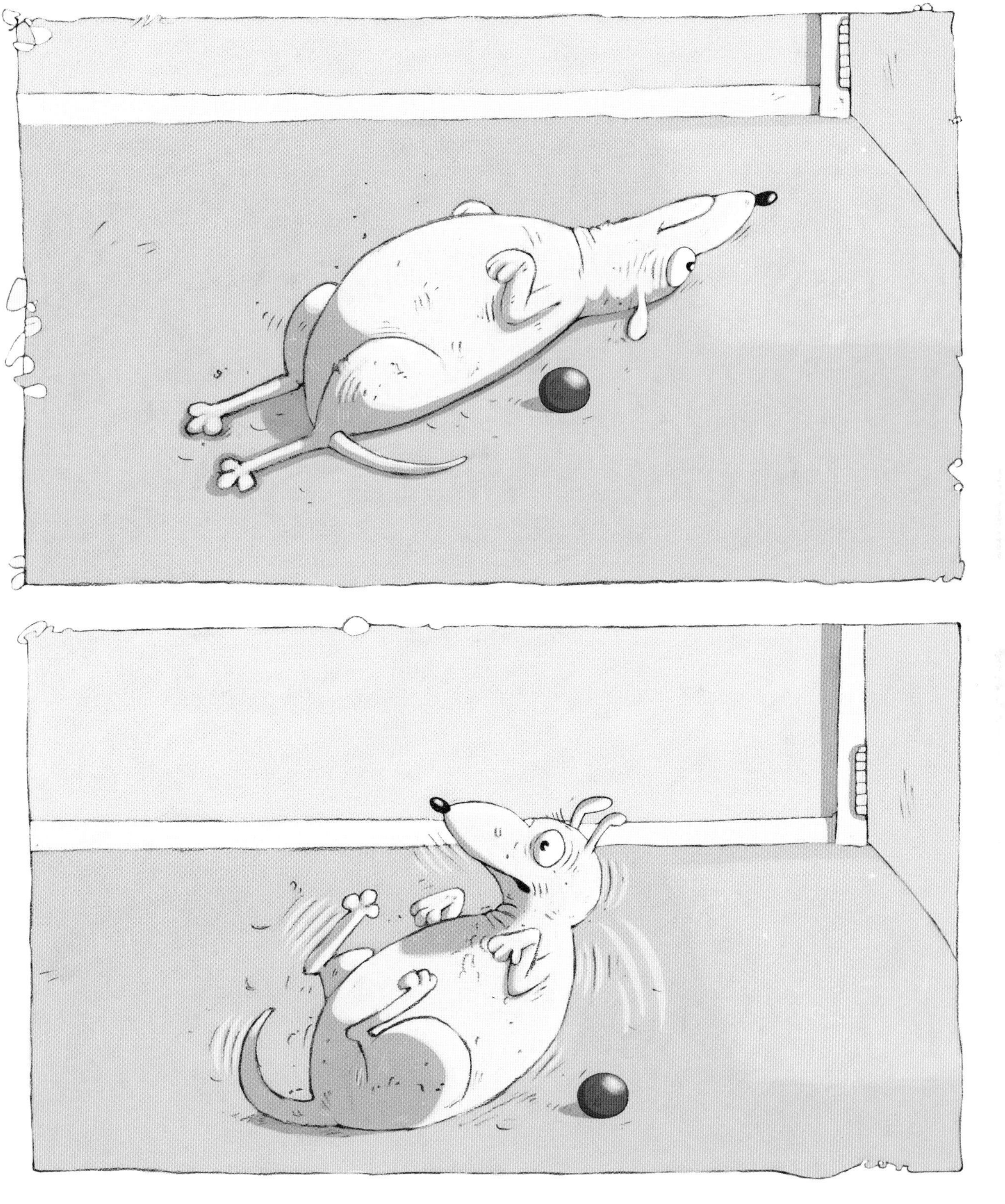

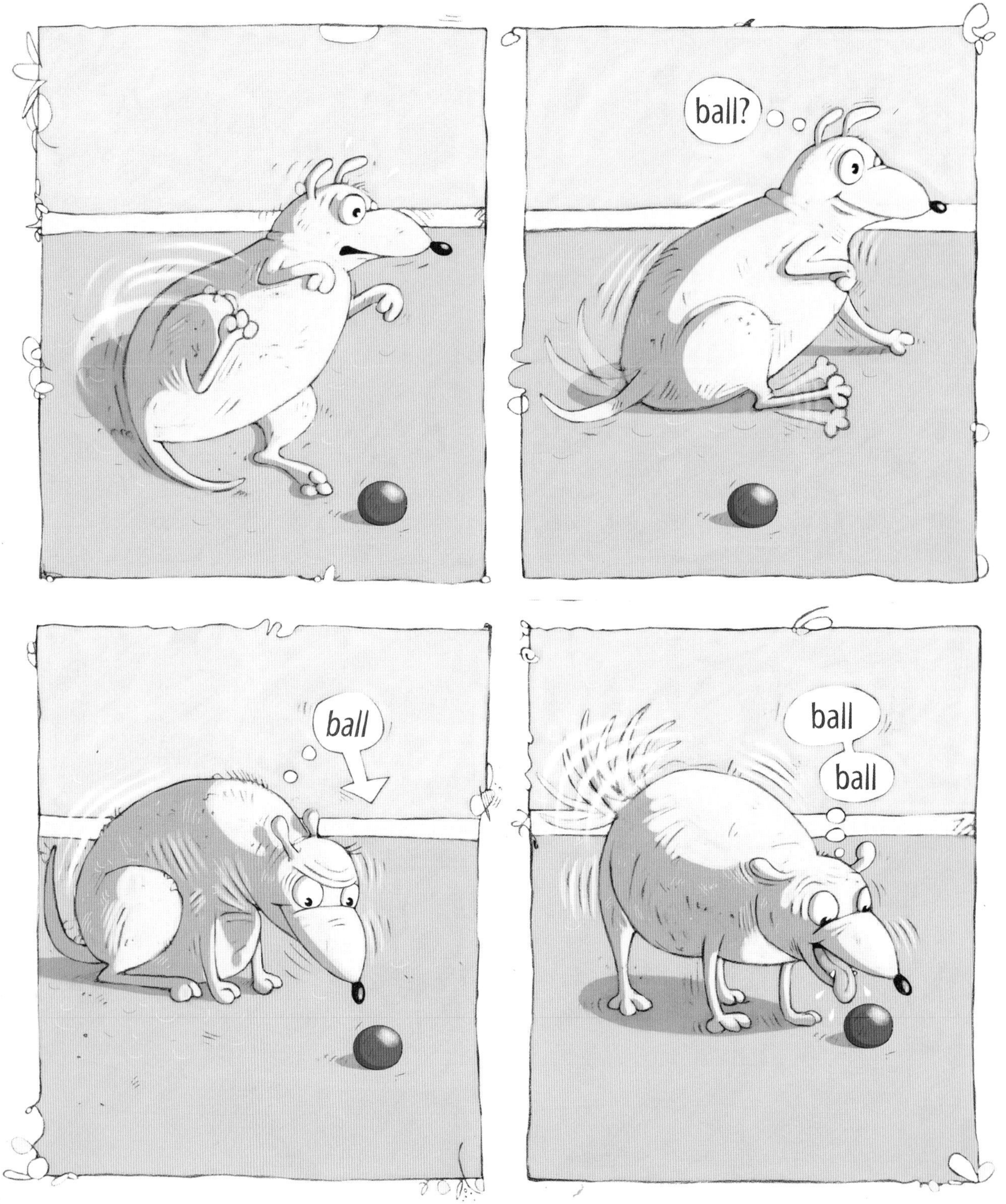
ball?
ball
ball
ball

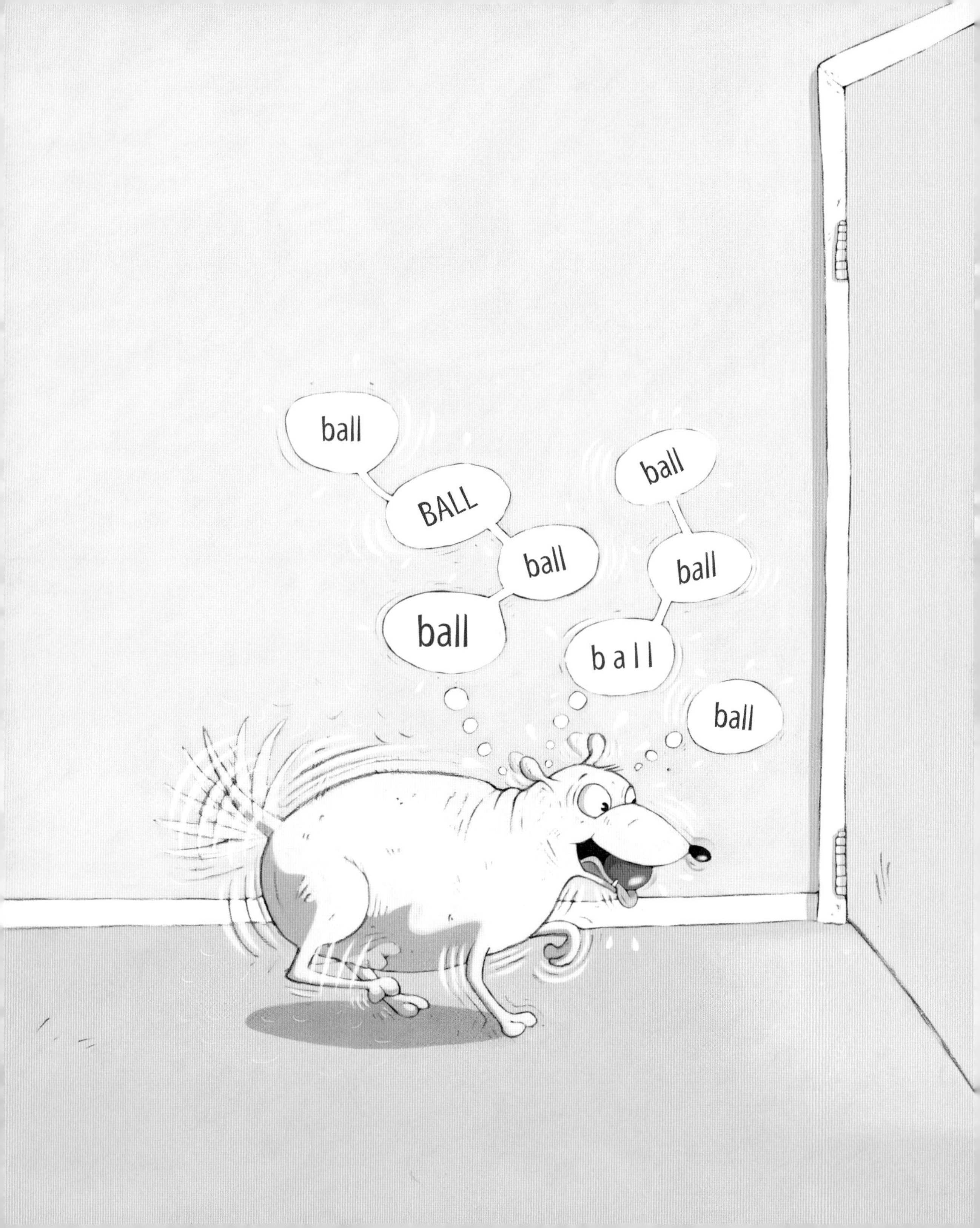
ball
BALL
ball
ball
ball
ball
b a l l
ball

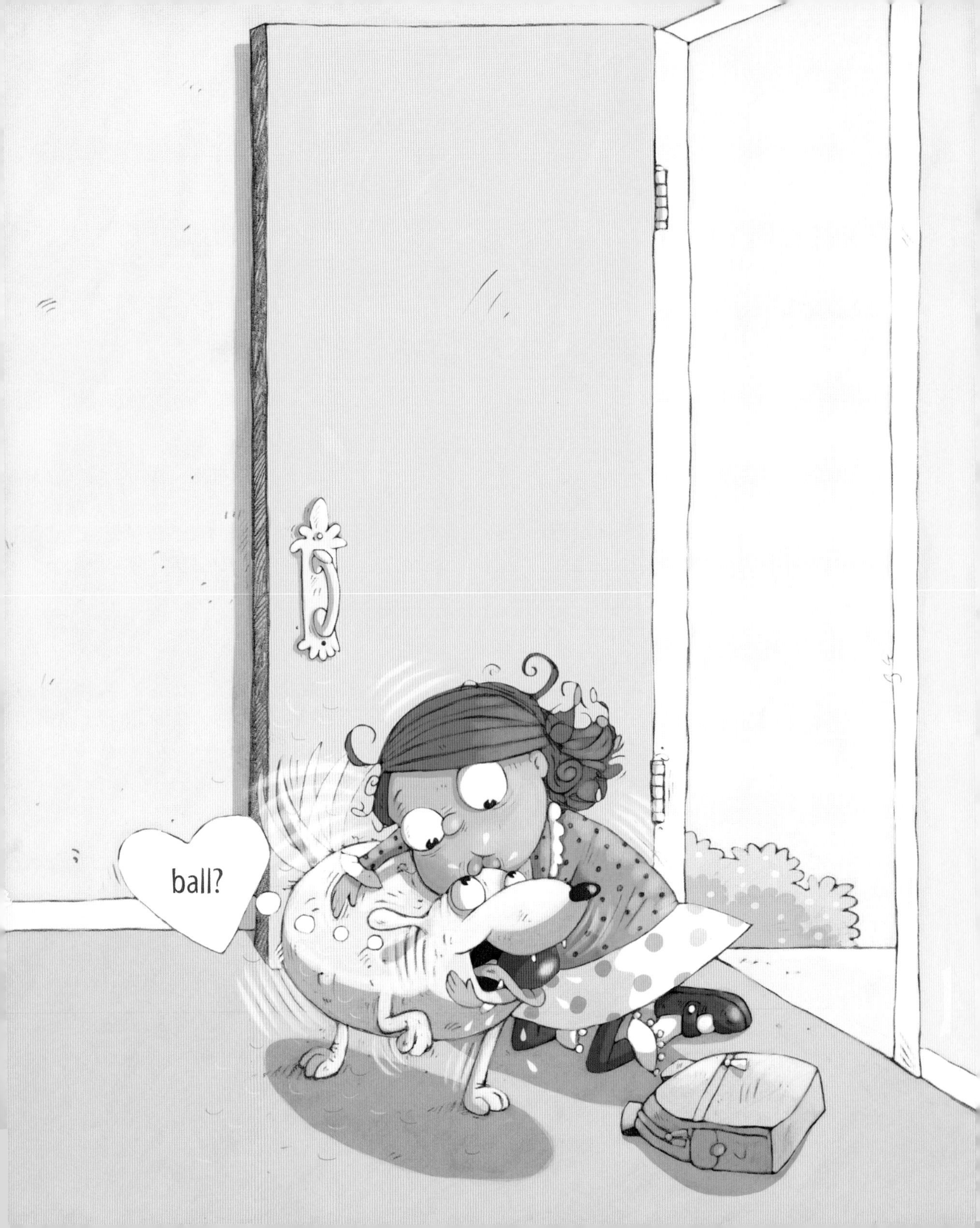
ball?

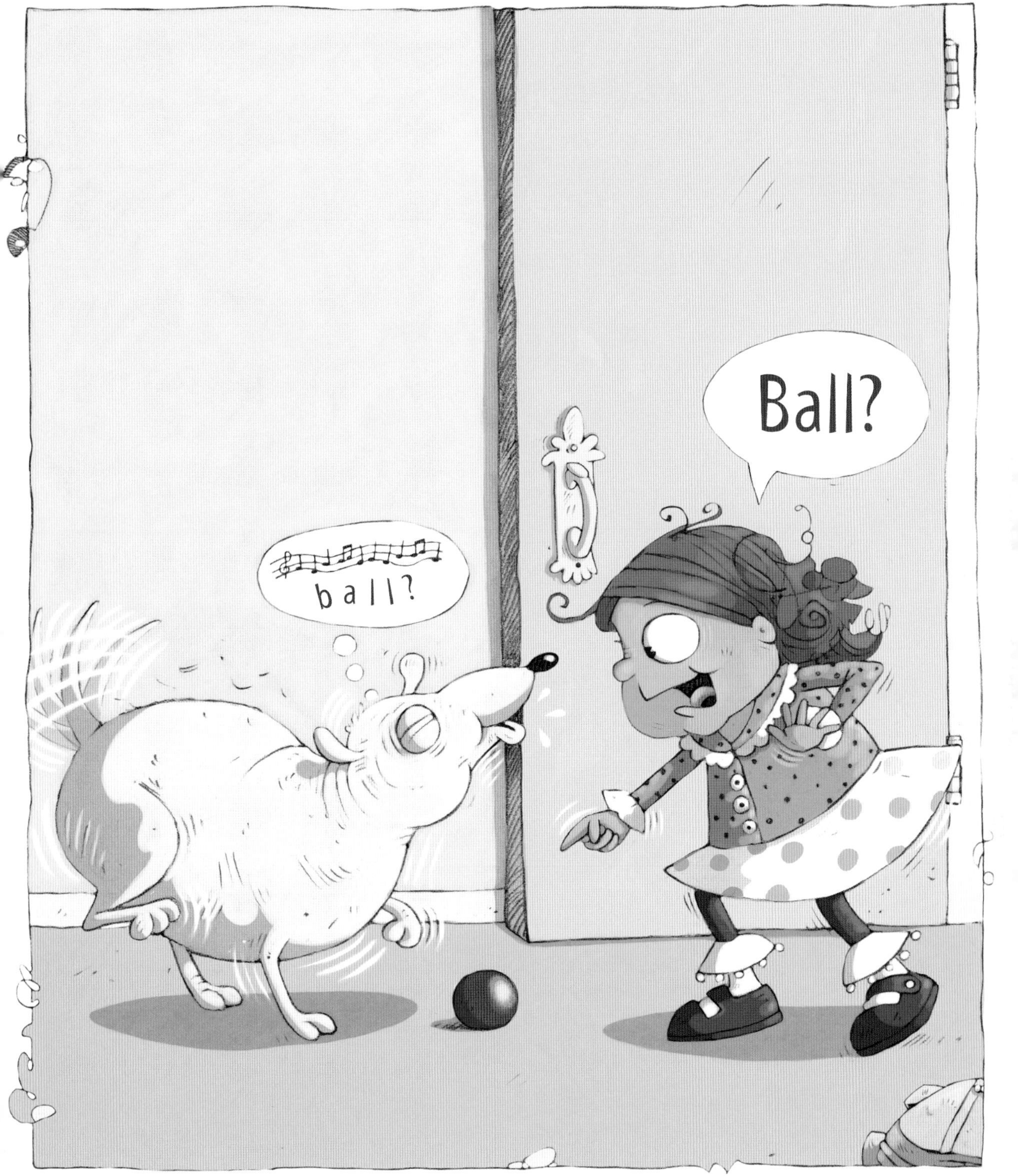
ball?
Ball?

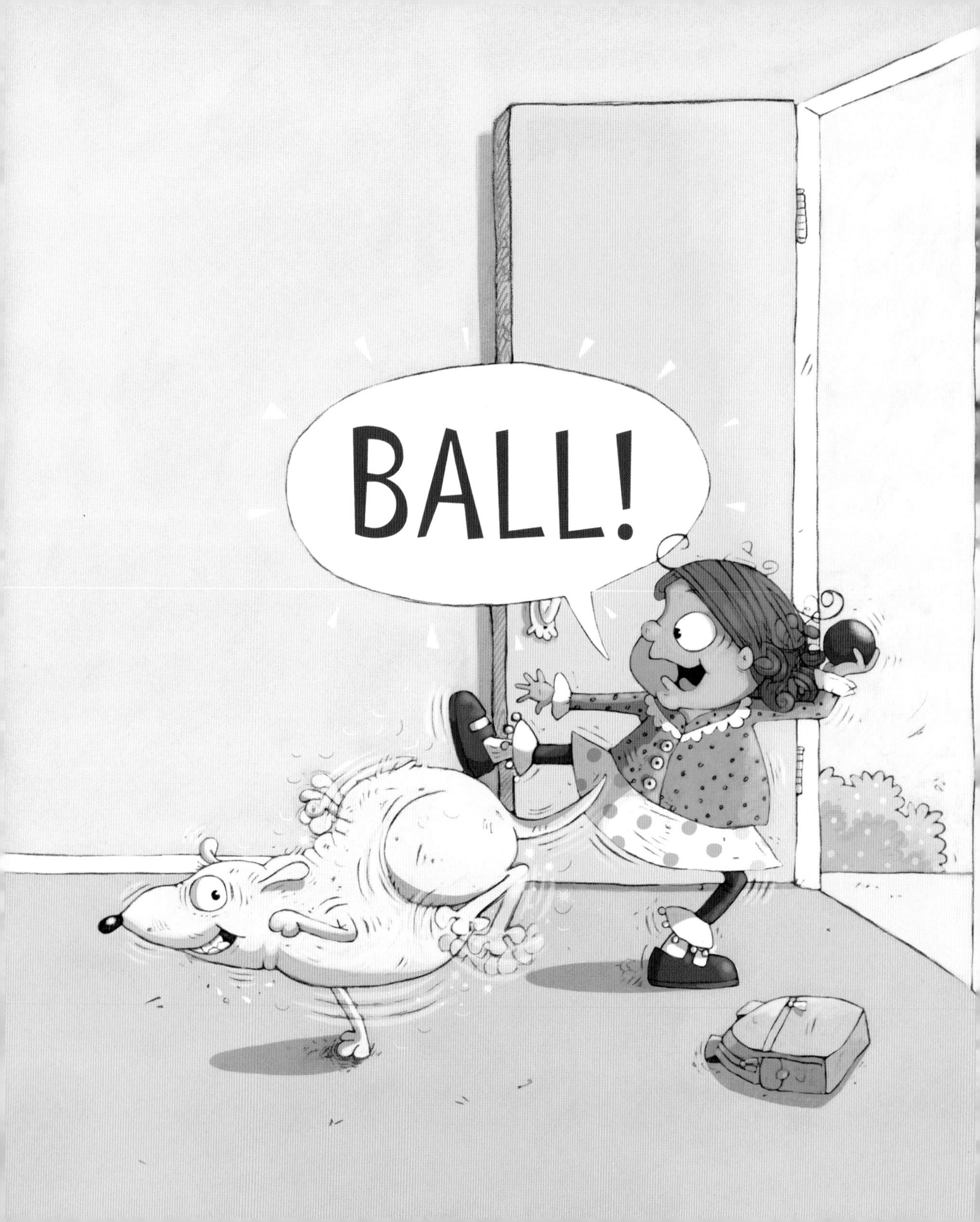
BALL!